THE OFF-KEY CONSPIRACY

SAM PARRISH

SWAMP SAGE BOOKS

BOOKS BY SAM PARRISH

The Off-Key Conspiracy

The Anagovia Trilogy

When the World Starts to Fray

When the Threads Unravel

When the Void Splits the Realm

For all my fellow adult beginners and ADHD hobby collectors. You're pretty cool.

CONTENTS

The Amberwood

The

Honey Gob

Leaves: Tea and Pages

Overhollow Fine Instruments

The City of Gr

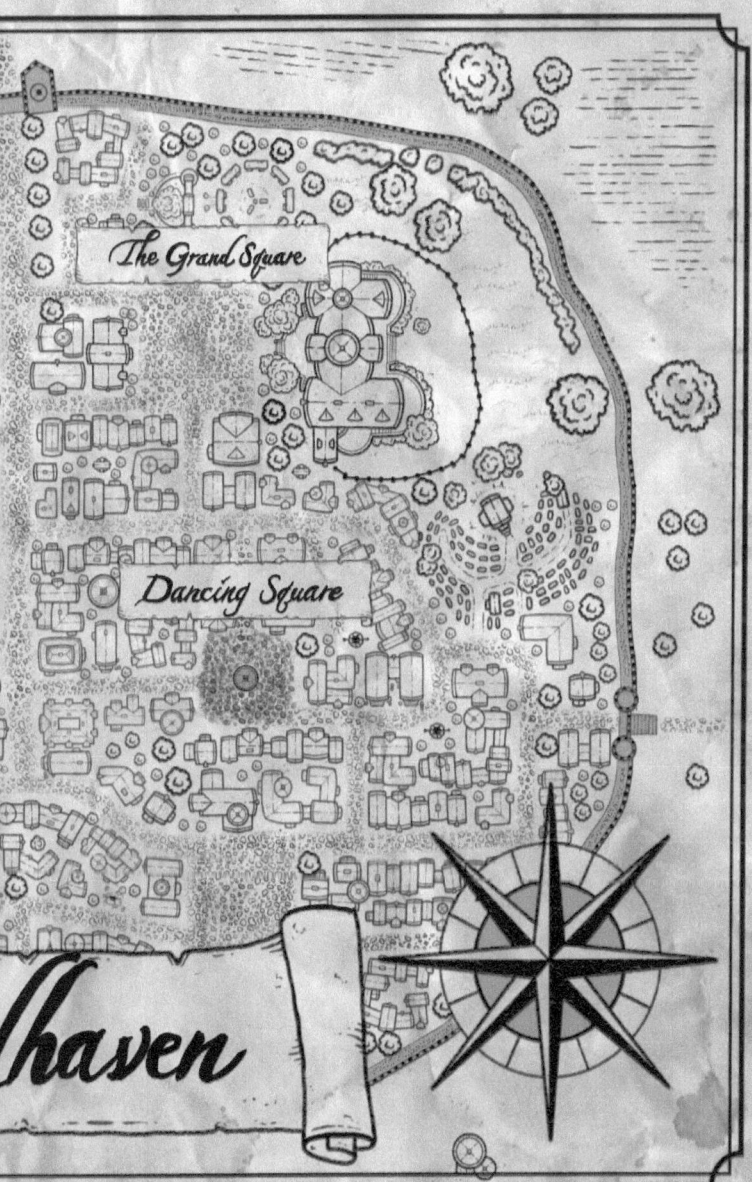

The Grand Square

Dancing Square

haven

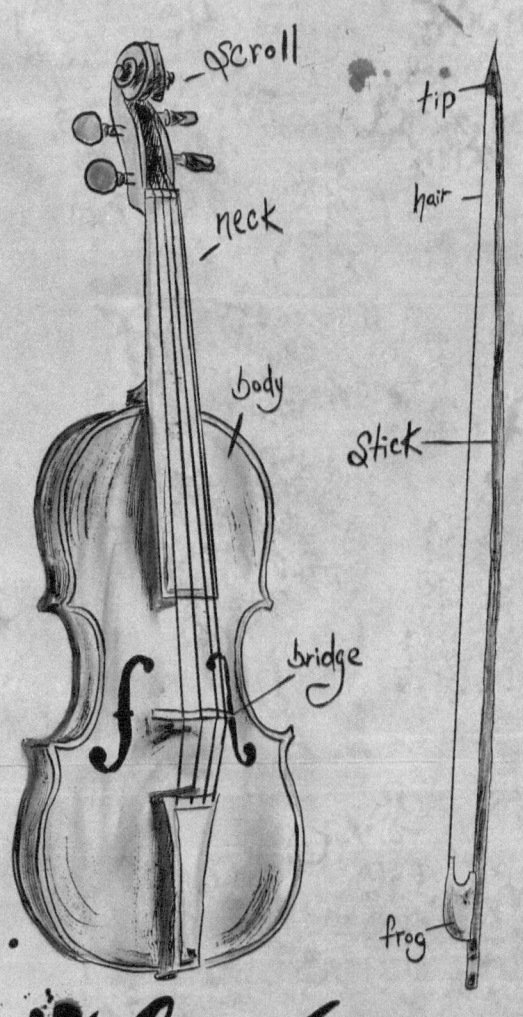

scroll

neck

body

bridge

f

tip

hair

stick

frog

Violin and Bow Parts

Chapter One

The Goldmead family had been the sole owners and operators of The Honey Goblet for generations. The tavern was, by all accounts, the finest establishment in all of Grandhaven. It was even said that the Goldmeads brewed the best mead in all of Sarenalyrd, right there in house with only local honey, fruit, and spices.

And it made Taeva Goldmead miserable.

She wasn't supposed to be there. Yes, it was her family's tavern, and yes, she'd lived there her entire life. She'd left months ago, though, and hadn't planned on coming back. But there she was, trudging down the stairs to the main floor, hollowed out and bored already even though the day hadn't truly started.

The sun was beginning to guild the streets of Grandhaven, so it was time to open The Honey Goblet for the day. She circled the large open space on the ground floor and pulled open the honey-yellow curtains. Early autumn sunshine spilled in through the large panes, flowing over the worn wooden floors with their mismatched rugs and warming the stone walls. Coals from the night before still glowed in the open stone hearth in the center of the room. She added some kindling and poked them back to life, then added a few more logs. Autumn hadn't gotten cold enough to need a roaring flame, but a little extra heat would be welcome.

She stood in the middle of the room, smoothing down her rust-colored skirt and casting one more glance around the room, making sure everything was in place and all the tables were clean. The tavern was perfect—cozy, warm, inviting—but goddesses, it got so dull. Her gaze landed on the stage opposite the bar, and her stomach gave an uncomfortable lurch. With a grimace, she turned away.

She should have been over it already. Instead, it felt like a cowardly retreat as she walked back to the front door and flipped the sign in the front window to *Open*.

She was settling onto her stool behind the wooden bar when her parents and Grams made their way down the stairs. Taeva took a deep breath and plastered a smile across her face. She knew it was a weak and wobbly one, but her family didn't comment.

"Ready for the day, honey?" her father asked, bright as the sunshine streaming through the windows. He was already rolling up the sleeves of his crisp white shirt, enthusiastic as ever.

"Of course! Hopefully we're busy," Taeva answered, trying to mirror some of his positivity.

He smiled wider, the corners of his eyes wrinkling behind his glasses. Then he ducked off into the kitchen behind the bar and vanished down into the cellar to start monitoring the progress of their seasonal meads.

"Busy would be best," Grams chimed in. She tied her aggressively neat and starched apron over her skirts—a sharp contrast to her wild grey hair.

"Good morning, dear," her mother said, the picture of contentment as she swept past on her way to the kitchen.

They all looked so happy, like there was nothing they'd rather do than spend another day running the tavern. Taeva had never shared their love for mead-making and business, though she often wished—especially since coming home—that she did. Things would have been so much easier.

Even though she didn't want to be there, she hadn't lied when she said she hoped they would be busy. If they had a lot of customers and she spent her day running back and forth with their orders, she'd have less time to think about the failure that brought her back to The Honey Goblet in the first place.

THE GODDESSES GRANTED HER THEIR FAVOR.

The postman came to drop off their mail, and their first group of customers wandered into The Honey Goblet right on his heels shortly after Taeva's mother and Grams got the fires started in the ovens. They kept streaming through the doors well into the late afternoon. Taeva took orders at the bar, rushing to keep the line short, a pleasant expression painted across her face. Once they seated themselves and their orders were ready, Taeva bustled to their tables and dropped them off. Then it was a simple, if chaotic, game of keeping their mugs and glasses full.

It was a well-practiced routine. She'd grown up helping in the tavern, slowly taking on more responsibilities as she got older. At twenty-two, she was so used to the flow of the day she could probably man the bar in her sleep.

It should have been a comfort when she came home four months ago, sliding back into a reliable routine like pulling on her favorite, slightly worn dress. It wasn't, though. It felt too much like failure. But she threw herself into the work. If she applied herself, paid the customers extra attention, and focused on each task like a wizard bent over a new spell, she could drown out everything else.

So that's what she did. By the time the worst of the lunchtime rush was over, she'd scuttled through the tables fast enough and often enough to work up a sweat. Pausing behind the bar, she rolled the sleeves of her dress up and tied her riot of blonde curls into a tail. It fluffed out immediately, trying to escape, but it was off her neck and shoulders at least.

It will have to do, she told herself. So many things would just have to do.

A lifted hand at one of the tables caught her attention. She glanced back to the bar and no one was waiting to order, so she ambled over with her practiced smile in place.

It was one of their regulars—a blacksmith from a few streets over and his two apprentices. The blacksmith, Bartley Smeltiron, was a burly, greyish-skinned half-orc with hands that looked like they could squash whole melons in their grasp. He also had some of the kindest eyes Taeva had ever seen. He gave her a toothy—and tusky—grin as she walked up. His two apprentices glanced her way with a nod and a wave but were too busy discussing the merits of different ores to pay her much mind. She still needed to learn their names.

"Is everything alright?" she asked. "Your meals should be done any moment now. I'm sorry if it's taking too long." *Chicken, fried in Grams's special batter. Side of this season's veggies. Same for all three.* The Honey Goblet's mead menu was much longer than the one for food, but she repeated their order to herself all the same.

"Not a problem at all," Bartley said in his gravelly voice. "I was wondering when your autumn mead will be back on the menu. The one with the pumpkin and spices added to it."

"You know, it should be soon." Taeva put her hands on

her hips. She checked for new customers one more time and, seeing none, said, "I'll go ask for you. And I'll check on your food while I'm at it."

"Thank you," Bartley said, then he turned back to his apprentices, who were still deep in discussion. "Oh no, absolutely not. You quench iron while it's that hot, and it'll explode." Taeva cringed at the thought of such a terrible accident and whisked away.

She looked through windows behind the bar as she walked up, but saw only her mother and Grams working away in the kitchen. That meant her father was still down in the cellar, fussing with his mead and his charts and his lists. She breezed through to the back of the kitchen, where a handrail cordoned off the stairs leading into the cellar.

Please don't do it, please don't, she repeated to herself as she trotted down the stairs. Taking a deep breath, she knocked on the door out of courtesy, then let herself in.

Kegs of mead covered three of the walls, from the stone floor to the wooden ceiling. The final wall was lined with shelves, bursting with three generations of notebooks, each one filled with information about mead and the family business. Three bar-height, round tables stood in the middle of the room. Her father sometimes held private tastings in the cool air of the cellar—they were always a big hit with couples looking to have an intimate evening. A lantern sat on each table, lending the space plenty of flickering, warm light.

Her father was tapping a new keg of mead, but straightened as she came in, brow creasing. She hardly ever went down into the cellar.

"Everything alright?" Tirson asked.

"Everything is great," she lied. "We've stayed super busy,

but I have a customer asking when the autumn mead will be ready."

"Taeva," Tirson started, disappointment already coloring his tone. "I've shown you the records enough times that you shouldn't have to ask." He crossed to the shelf and pulled one of the notebooks down, then brought it to the table closest to her. "Come here." He sounded as exasperated as Taeva felt.

She met him at the table as he flipped through to the most recently updated page in his book. At first glance, it looked like a mad scrawl, more complex than any sheet music Taeva had ever seen. There was a chart filled with dates and numbers, notes written sideways in the margins, things underlined and scratched out. It all made sense to Tirson Goldmead, though, and he launched into the same lecture Taeva had heard since she was old enough to read, stroking his blonde beard with one hand and pointing at figures with the other.

This is why she'd left. Not because of her father, but because of the tavern. It was *painfully* boring. Mead-making was ninety percent waiting and ten percent measuring, and it made her so fidgety she wanted to crawl out of her skin. The business side of the tavern was even worse—nothing but numbers. A wall of numbers and figures that threatened to collapse if even one digit was wrong.

It was nothing like music or magic. And nothing like the adventures she'd read about in her books—though real-life adventures hadn't turned out like the stories either.

Taeva jerked herself away from that train of thought and focused back on what her father was saying with desperate attention. She couldn't let her mind wander like that. It would only depress her more. She'd tried making her life about music and magic. It hadn't worked. It was past time for her to let it go.

Buried deep in her father's lecture, she caught that the autumn mead should be ready in another week. She pasted her smile back in place, hoping it didn't look too much like relief, and took a couple of steps back toward the door.

"I'll let them know." She took another step, trying not to wilt under Tirson's glare. He didn't like being interrupted. "Can't keep them waiting!"

She rushed back up the stairs, feeling like she'd barely escaped. Bartley and his apprentices' meals were ready, and she scooped them up as she fled through the kitchen. She delivered the food and the good news about the mead, made sure their drinks were full, then slumped back onto her stool behind the bar.

Her mask had fallen; she felt it in the aching relief in her cheeks. She couldn't bring herself to put it back in place. Her eyes drifted back to the stage. It was just a small platform, only one step high and barely large enough for a few musicians to perform without feeling cramped, but it seemed to swell in size until it filled the room. Later that night, there would be musicians performing and people dancing. And she would be stuck here, working and watching it all.

She sighed. It was funny how one conversation could turn the day sour.

"Your father pestered you again, didn't he?"

Taeva jumped and whirled to find her grandmother wiping her hands on her apron and leaning against the bar top beside her. She'd been so lost in her melancholy she hadn't noticed the older woman walk up.

"He kind of did," Taeva said with a sigh. "I don't think I'll ever be able to make sense of his records, though."

Grams snorted. "It would take a gaggle of wizards to decode that mess. His father would have a fit if he could see it. Still, his mead is wonderful, and the tavern stays open. So there's good information in there."

Taeva deflated further. "I know, I know. I should work harder to figure it all out."

Grams's lined face softened under her wild cloud of hair. She rubbed Taeva's back. "Only if you want to, sugar. We were all sad that you didn't want to stay to take on the business, but that doesn't mean much. You have to find something you enjoy. Your father loves the mead and The Honey Goblet. You love music and magic. We just want you to be safe and happy."

Music and magic.

Taeva gave up resisting and flopped onto the counter. "Grams, I haven't touched the violin in four months," she whined. "I don't know that I even want to play anymore."

Grams squeezed her into a fierce hug. She smelled like thyme and clean linen. "I know. And I so miss your playing. But you'll figure out your true calling, dearie. And we'll all support you, every step of the way."

Taeva sank into her grandmother's hug, desperately willing that to be true.

*T*aeva clung to her grandmother's words for comfort for the rest of the day. They managed to carry her through the beginning of the dinner surge but petered out as soon as the band arrived for the evening and started setting up.

They were a trio, dressed in matching motley vests of red and gold with bright white, ruffled shirts underneath. The oldest of the bunch, a man so pale he looked like he'd never seen the sun, was their drummer. He sat up drums of various sizes in an arc around a low stool, then sat and busied himself with checking the tension on the hide drum-heads. The lutist and flutist—a pair of elves with deep brown skin and dark hair who looked like they must've been sisters—only had to tune their instruments to prepare, and mingled with the customers while the drummer made adjustments.

Taeva avoided them like they were spreading lycanthropy. It helped her keep her focus on her work—at least, for the most part. It all fell apart, though, as soon as they played their first notes. Then they became impossible to ignore.

She tried her best to focus on the customers. She really did. She engaged them in short conversations any time she dropped off an order or a refilled mug. It made the customers feel valued and at home, yes, but it also gave her information to memorize. Tucking all the little details they fed her away helped keep the music planted firmly in the background.

Helped, but didn't succeed entirely.

Snatches of song kept breaking through. She'd turn away from a table after dropping off food, and a particularly well-played bit of vibrato from the flute would ring through her like she was resonating and producing the sounds herself. She'd take payment at the counter, and in the middle of recounting the coin, a particularly delicious chord on the lute made her head feel like it was buzzing. At one point, she stood arrested in the doorway to the kitchen as the trio started up a triumphant, upbeat piece in D major.

Taeva recognized the tune by the third note. *That will get the people dancing,* she thought as she tried to shrug it off. She forced herself back to the counter to take a drink order.

She was right. People crowded the small open space in front of the stage, twirling in a riot of color. They laughed, stomped, and clamped with the drums, and ended in a chorus of *Huzzah!* right on time with the musicians.

It was a great performance.

It was torture.

It wasn't the first time her father had hired musicians to play since she'd been home. It was good business for a tavern. People loved music, they loved mead, and they loved the two together even more. People were more likely to linger and order another drink—or five—if they were dancing and having a good time. She couldn't fault her family for taking advantage of a proven tactic. But after her father's disappointed lecture and Grams mentioning music *and* magic, she was having a harder time coping than normal.

She was contemplating if she could get away with

escaping upstairs early when another customer walked up to the bar.

Just one more, Taeva told herself as she walked over, ready to take the newcomer's order.

Taeva hadn't seen this customer in the tavern before, but she looked familiar. Her long, dark hair was braided into a crown, revealing her delicately pointed half-elf ears. She wore the dark purple and blue robes of the Grandhaven Academy of Wizardry, and the colors set off her deeply tanned skin, making it seem to glow in the candlelight. She looked to be about Taeva's age, though she was bent like an old woman under the weight of her backpack.

The young half-elf perked up when she saw Taeva. "Oh, I was right. I do recognize you. Taeva, right?"

"Yes, that's me," Taeva said, leaning into her well-prac-ticed manners, even though she had to fight not to squirm under the other woman's penetrating gaze. "I'm terribly sorry, but you have me at a bit of a disadvantage."

"Overhollow. Leena Overhollow. You and your parents used to come into my parents' shop every now and then. You likely saw them more than me."

Taeva fought not to groan as the name clicked into place. Overhollow Fine Instruments. Another reminder of her life before she'd left, failed, then had to come crawling back home. What a truly terrible day this was shaping up to be.

"Of course! I'm sorry I didn't recognize you!" Taeva said, her smile feeling only a little brittle.

"How is your playing coming along?" Leena asked, almost barreling over Taeva's apology. "Violin, right? I used to help keep records for the shop. I seem to remember the name Goldmead in the books for work on a violin."

"Um, yes—"

"Are you incorporating magic with your playing? Bards

are fascinating. Such similar spells to what we learn at the Academy but such a different approach."

Taeva's chest suddenly felt too tight. She cleared her throat. "What can I get for you? We still have some of our summer mead available. It's made with wildflower honey. Pairs well with the chicken pot pie."

Leena blinked, confusion clear on her face. "Sure," she answered, then ordered exactly what Taeva had suggested. Taeva took Leena's coin and busied herself with preparing her drink order. It embarrassed her to have been so awkward, but she was relieved to escape.

Leena caught her again, though, when Taeva delivered her food. The wizard had sat herself at the furthest table from the stage and arranged a shocking number of books across its surface. It was clear she wasn't there for company.

"The background noise is a nice change of pace," she explained when Taeva cocked a brow. "And I didn't mean to make you feel awkward. I always forget that most people have no idea what we get up to at the Academy."

Taeva could have laughed as she handed Leena her bowl and silverware. The half-elf was so far off the mark it was a comfort. She searched the table, trying to find a safe place among the sprawl of books to put Leena's drink. Her eyes landed on a battered copy of *The Paladin and the Necromancer*. She moved closer, her eyes lighting up.

Taeva gasped. "Is this a first edition? One of the ones that were penned by the unknown author themselves?"

Leena paused in her efforts to rearrange the table. "No, I'm afraid not. Just a well-loved fake. I'm in the middle of rereading it."

"This is one of my absolute favorites." Taeva put her hand on the cover, smiling.

"Mine too! I'm almost back to the part where Mortica learns the necromancer's true name."

Taeva nodded enthusiastically as she replayed the plot twist in her mind. "I didn't see that part coming at all. Completely blind-sided."

"My older brother spoiled it for me," Leena said, rolling her eyes. "I should have burned his hair off for that. Speaking of mysteries and plot twists, did you hear about the murder?"

"The *murder?*" Taeva echoed, stunned.

Leena nodded, then took her tankard from Taeva's hand and sipped her mead. "Lord Elyk Amberwood was murdered in his own home sometime overnight, and three of his personal guard were badly wounded. I'm surprised you didn't hear about it already working in here."

"We do catch a lot of gossip, that's true," Taeva mused. "But now that you mention it, no one from the Watch has been in today, and a handful of Watchmen are regulars. We see them almost every day."

"They're probably all too busy to even eat. When someone as powerful as Lord Amberwood is killed, it sends all the other nobles into a panic. And when they panic, it becomes everyone's problem. They're probably all clamoring at the Head Watchmen's office, demanding the killer be caught and executed immediately. They never do like to be reminded that they're mortal," Leena said with an indelicate snort.

"Do they have any idea who might have done it?" Taeva asked, thoroughly distracted from work. She'd always loved mystery stories. Guilt pricked at her—this wasn't a story; this involved real people—but she couldn't help but be drawn in.

"Not a single clue," Leena answered around a mouthful

of chicken. "Or at least nothing that had made its way to the Academy when I left. The only possible witnesses would have been the guards, and none of them saw a thing."

"He was close to the king, wasn't he? Amberwood?" Taeva asked, trying to place the noble in her mind. She'd had occasion to meet a few of them *before* but always had a hard time with their names.

"Yes. Very. So I'm sure the king is bothering the Watch, too. But you don't cling to power like Amberwood did without making a wagonload of enemies along the way." Leena wagged her finger like she was giving a lecture.

A customer a few tables over waved for Taeva's attention. "Well," she said, starting to excuse herself. "Tybrecht Wolfstone is a great Head Watchman. He's been in here a few times, though I don't think he gets much time to relax. It seems like he's always on a case. He'll figure it out. Wave me over or catch me at the bar if you need anything else. Enjoy your meal."

Taeva filled orders and refilled drinks for the rest of the evening and didn't realize until she laid down that night that she hadn't thought about music again. Not even once. She'd been pondering—and worrying—over the murder. It wasn't for her to sort out, though. And she was sure the Head Watchman would keep trouble from their door.

Chapter
Three

*T*he next morning promised to bring with it the same mundane routine that had tormented Taeva for the last four months, but there was one notable exception. Taeva opened the tavern, letting in the sunshine, then stoked the fire and lit the candles. The Honey Goblet was the same warm, welcoming place as always, and the same shadows that haunted Taeva still clung to the corners. But there had been a shift of some kind, and she didn't notice them as much.

She was still thinking about the murder. So much, in fact, that she worried she was becoming as macabre as a necromancer. But it was a distraction from the miasma of failure she'd been living in, so she let herself dwell on it perhaps a little too much.

When a group of Watchmen came into the tavern toward the end of the lunchtime rush—a trio of regulars whom she knew by name—she was inexcusably excited. She cursed to herself when her mom beat her to the counter to take their orders, but she hovered in the kitchen, waiting for their food to be dished out so she would be the one to deliver it. She didn't *need* an excuse to go up to the table to talk to the Watchmen, but if her father popped upstairs, she'd rather look busy and avoid any possible lectures.

"You seem to be in a better mood today, sugar," Grams said as she added a generous touch of black pepper to the lemony pan sauce she made to go over grilled fish. "What's got you so worked up?"

"I want to talk to the Watch about Lord Amberwood's murder." It didn't pay to try to lie to Grams. She had an almost magical ability to suss out the truth.

Grams gave an exaggerated grimace. "Ugly business, that. I hope you're not fretting over it too much. I'd bet a fair bit of coin it was politically motivated. All those nobles with all that money, fighting each other all day long—*tch*. Glad it's not me." She drizzled sauce over the waiting fish, then added the dish to a tray already laden with food. "This is for the Watch. And tell them they can have one free refill on the house for working so hard. Off you go!"

Taeva wound her way through the tables, balancing the heavy tray between her shoulder and both her hands—a move she'd seen her mother use ever since she was a child. As she drew up to the table, she caught the word *murder* and had to rein in her delight. The Watchmen kept up their discussion as she started handing out their meals, not bothered in the least that she'd overhear. They all still wore their uniforms, fitted black coats with formal tails that hit mid-thigh, though they'd unbuttoned them. They must have just gotten off duty. Taeva found herself stalling, moving slower than normal so she could gather more information.

Groslig, a half-orc with skin the same shade of blue as the noon sky, complained. "I know there's a big to-do over it, and there should be, but keeping us so late after our shift rubs me the wrong way. I could have been briefed when I got in tomorrow night."

"They'll probably brief us again then, too," Torressa answered wryly. Unlike most elves, who were tall and lean, she was tall and broad. Taeva would wager good coin that Torressa was just as strong as her half-orc counterpart.

Taeva placed the last dish in front of the quietest one of the three, who nodded his thanks. A pale, unassuming human with nice but forgettable features, Len was the type who noticed—and filed away—much more than he let on.

"Does the Head Watchman have any idea who did it?" Taeva asked, tucking the now-empty tray under one arm.

Len snorted, but it was Torressa who answered. "Not a clue. We have precious little information. It's like the killer cut their way out of the Amberwood home and then dissolved into the night."

Groslig groaned. "I hadn't even considered they might be some kind of magic user."

"You should have," Len answered, taking a sip of his mead.

"We'll probably never find them if that's the case," Groslig added.

Taeva knew she shouldn't pry—she was merely a barmaid at this point, after all. She wasn't an adventurer, and this wasn't her quest. But she couldn't help herself. She'd found something less painful to fixate on, and she was loathe to let it go when it came as such a relief.

"What information do you have so far?" she asked, hoping it sounded casual.

"Like I said, it's not much," Torressa answered. "Most of the stab wounds on Amberwood and his guards were on their right, and the slashing ones run from their left to their right." She mimed the motions with her fork held in her left hand. "So we're assuming the killer was left-handed."

"Or so skilled with a sword that they can use it well in either hand," Len added dryly. "Or using a spelled blade and not touching it at all."

"Why are you like this?" Groslig asked, glaring at Len. Taeva snorted, earning a quick wink from the half-orc.

"And we know the culprit was wounded," Torressa said, holding up a hand like she could block out the other two and their bickering. "There's blood leading from the body to where the guards were found. Not a lot, but it's there. Amberwood got at least one cut in, goddesses grant him rest."

"Rest well," Taeva chimed with the other two guards.

"Could have also been blood dripping off the murder weapon," Len said after the short prayer.

"Now you're just being negative," Groslig said with a glare. "You know it was too much for that."

Len shrugged and focused on his meal.

Torressa gave Taeva an exasperated look, pushing a hand through her short-cropped brown hair. Taeva grinned back at the elf. The trio argued like family, and it always brightened her day to listen to them bicker. The subject of the day was a little heavier than what they normally discussed, but the way they banded together against the challenge was wonderful to see. It reminded Taeva of the heroic guilds in her novels. Their bonds always strengthened through their struggles.

Not at all like the bonds between me and the Reavers, she thought. The shadows loomed a little darker, but she pushed them back into the corners. She'd stay busy. She wouldn't give herself time to wallow.

"If you all need anything, wave me over. I'll check on you in a bit." She patted the table and left to help the rest of the late lunchers.

Taeva made her rounds through the tavern, delivering refills and wiping down the tables after customers left. Her imagination took the reins and ran off with her like a spooked horse. While she worked, she conjured up a comically stereotypical murderer in her mind. A man, twirling his oily mustache with a gnarled finger and holding a chipped, rusty dagger in his left hand. The character in her mind limped away from the murder scene carrying a bag of gold, vanishing into the night and cackling.

Taeva froze in the middle of wiping down the bar, then rushed back to the Watchmen's table.

"Did they steal anything?" she blurted out.

They all looked at her, confused. Their conversation had long since turned to other matters.

"Who?" Groslig asked.

"The killer."

Understanding dawned across the half-orc's features. "Ah. They didn't. According to Amberwood's widow, not a single thing is missing."

Taeva's brow creased, and she pushed an errant blonde curl out of her face. "That's strange, isn't it? They must have been after something."

"It's possible, but right now the Watch is ruling it as an assassination attempt that took a turn, not a theft gone wrong. Purely political," Torressa said.

Taeva's mind whirled, her mental image of the killer shifting into something less comical and more menacing.

"Is there anything we need to do? Something we should look out for? Can we help somehow?" she asked, suddenly worried about political schemes that would swallow all of Grandhaven.

She grimaced at her own panic, though the Watchmen didn't seem to notice how her voice jumped half an octave. She knew, deep down, that she was worrying over this like a dog with a bone for absolutely no reason. She wasn't going to solve the case, wouldn't be helping anyone. But she couldn't resist. She was hooked, and her brain wouldn't let it go. Her thoughts would keep wandering back to the case at every spare moment. It had been a blessing when she needed to hunker down and learn a new, complex piece of music. Now it was more of a curse.

"Even I will admit it was most likely political," Len said. "I doubt anyone other than nobility has any cause for worry." He dropped a few coins on the table as the other two drained their drinks.

"Amberwood's funeral is tomorrow morning. Reckon we'll see you there," Groslig said, and they all stood. "The king is *encouraging* everyone to attend." The lilt he added to the word 'encouraging' spoke volumes. The entire city would be expected to attend.

"We'll probably be there, then." She waved them out the door. "Enjoy your day!"

She turned back to the table and started cleaning it up, her mind wandering far, far away from her work. She hoped they were right, and the attack had been motivated by some secret rivalry between Grandhaven nobles. She hoped it stayed far away from The Honey Goblet. As much as she didn't want to be there, she couldn't stand the thought of something happening to it or, goddesses forbid, her family.

Chapter Four

he following morning found the Goldmead family walking through the streets of Grand-haven on their way to the public funeral.

Dawn flooded the cobbled streets with the kind of warm, buttery light that promised golden and mild autumn days for weeks to come. It spilled over the stone walls of the shops and homes around them, making everything look like it was basking in the glow of a hearth fire.

The charm was lost on Grams, though.

"Strongly encouraged. Bah! Why don't they just say it's required instead of trying to sugarcoat everything?" she grumbled. "We'll have to open late because of this!"

"King Rouric only wants to make sure we all know he cares," Taeva's mother said with the air of someone who'd repeated this a hundred times already. And she had. She pinned a few loose hairs back into her greying strawberry-blonde bun. She normally only pulled her hair half-up to get it out of her face, but she had done it up as neatly as she could for the occasion.

Taeva hadn't even bothered trying to force hers into order. Going outside into the wind this time of year fluffed it into a blonde cloud no matter what she did.

Grams rolled her eyes. "Elawin, no Dragonsbane king has ever cared overmuch about what the people think."

"Mother," Tirson hissed, alarmed.

"Don't worry, dear. They aren't going to nab an old woman. I'll just pretend I'm senile."

Taeva laughed. Grams was as sharp as any knife. She couldn't pass for senile, no matter how hard she tried. No one would ever believe her.

The crowd around them grew the closer they got to the Grand Square until they were walking elbow to elbow, reaching for each other occasionally to make sure they weren't pushed apart. It looked like the entire city, or close to it, had taken the king's word very seriously. They poured into the square in front of the palace from all directions like a lazy river.

The Grand Square spanned nearly a quarter of a mile in every direction, all of it neatly cobbled and meticulously maintained. The palace, with its spires and sweeping buttresses, took up the entire eastern side. Its many stained glass windows and gilded doorways glittered in the morning light. The other three sides were occupied by a mixture of glitzy shops and the homes of various nobles. They'd all been fashioned after the palace, but their architects made sure not to seem like they were trying to overpower its grandeur. It made them all look like smaller replicas of the king's home, even if they were more lavish than anywhere most people would ever visit.

Taeva and her family wedged through the crowd, looking for somewhere to stand. They passed the Amberwood home on their left, and Taeva felt her gaze drawn to it like a seeking spell. It didn't look much different from the other nobles' homes around the square. The stained glass set in the doors and at the tops of the windows had a slightly different design but had clearly been made in the same time and fashion as the ones in the palace and the other manors. The only thing that set it apart was the curling golden *A* above the doors. Walking past it made the hair on the back of Taeva's neck stand on end. Knowing the violence that happened there three days ago, she couldn't help but imagine ghosts in the windows, glaring out at everyone in the square. Surely such a violent act left some kind of mark behind. It sent a chill skittering up her spine. If there was something left over in the manor, the Head Wizards would find it.

Her father stopped them a few buildings down, thankfully, in front of a florist shop. The windows showcased arrangements of flowers shipped from all across Sarenalyrd, some so elaborate they were clearly meant to decorate the palace.

"Well, hello," said a familiar voice.

Leena pushed through the crowd and stopped in front of the Goldmeads. She was dressed in her uniform robes again, a swath of purple and blue, and bent under the weight of her bulging backpack.

"Leena Overhollow!" Elawin exclaimed. She hugged the half-elf with the same enthusiasm she used to greet family. "The Academy of Wizardry—how wonderful! How's your mother?"

"Doing well and staying very busy in the shop," Leena answered. "She might be able to retire soon, since my older brother's apprenticeship with her will be over in a few months."

"Knowing her, she probably still won't," Taeva's mother said, smiling. "I miss going to the shop and visiting with her."

The comment was in no way directed at Taeva, but it felt like an arrow shot straight for her heart all the same. She winced, then struggled to school her face back into a neutral and pleasant expression.

A confused look spread across Leena's face. "You haven't been to the..." She trailed off, her eyes shifting to Taeva and snagging. Something flickered across her expression, and she straightened, turning to Tirson instead. "I've been wanting to catch you at the tavern, but can I ask a few questions about mead making?"

It was the most effective change of subject possible. Taeva's father latched on to any topic that fell into the mead-making category with all the tenacity of an ogre with its food. Leena asked some basic questions, getting small details wrong, and Tirson jumped in, cutting the young wizard off mid-sentence to correct her.

Taeva breathed a sigh of relief. Whether Leena was motivated out of sympathy or pity, it didn't matter. She'd steered everyone away from Taeva's music and, more importantly, the lack thereof. She listened to her father ramble until a flash of light and a single clear note rang out over the crowd from the front of the palace.

Everyone fell silent as multicolored lights drifted up until they were at the height of the shorter palace towers. They grouped together, condensing until a perfect copy of King Rouric Dragonsbane XI's face floated in front of his palace gates. The Dragonsbanes were half-elves, and the current king looked exactly like what Taeva would expect of royalty. His strong jaw was covered in a neat, dark brown beard. Piercing dark eyes looked out over the crowd with such focus it made her wonder if he could see through the illusion. His pointed ears were hidden beneath shoulder-length hair that fell in neat waves.

"People of Grandhaven," he intoned, his voice magically amplified to carry over the crowd. "I wish we'd gathered today under happier circumstances..."

Taeva tried her best to listen to his speech, but when the

king started going on about the devastation of Lord Amber-wood's death and how it would be impossible to fill his place as a loyal advisor, her focus drifted away. It was then that she noticed the flash of a sage green cloak moving through the crowd.

Taeva's heart leapt into her throat, and for a moment, she forgot how to breathe. She stood rooted in place, skin flushing hot and cold at the same time, her pulse pounding in her ears in an aggressive accelerando.

The green flash came again. She held her breath, but it only was the hair of a gnome Watchmen stalking through the crowd. The relief that swept over Taeva was so profound she almost wilted.

A second Watchman followed behind the gnome—a human man, stubble dusting his dark cheeks and his keen eyes narrowed. They both pushed through the crowd, passing right in front of Taeva and her family, each with a hand on their swords, studying every person they passed. Further to their right, a pale purple female half-orc—also a Watchman—pushed through the crowd, glaring at everyone like they were mere moments away from committing a crime.

Taeva tapped Leena's shoulder. "What are the guards doing?" she asked.

The other woman peered at the crowd, frowning. She muttered something under her breath, and her dark eyes lit from within with a faint purple glow. Taeva didn't catch the words Leena muttered, but she recognized the spell. Leena was looking *through* the crowd now, able to pinpoint whatever she wanted. She scowled, her eyes following things through the crowd that Taeva couldn't see.

"I think they're looking for the killer," Leena muttered.

The king's speech reached an end with him stressing the

importance of honoring the sacrifices of the fallen noble and his wounded guards and cooperating with the Watch to ensure the city's safety. The giant illusion of his face winked out of existence, and the crowd was dismissed.

"Humph," Grams scoffed. "Same as every royal funeral speech I've ever heard! And I've lived long enough to have heard more than a few."

"Mother..." Tirson said, exasperated.

"What? It's the truth! We were all thinking it. I'm just the only one to actually say it."

"If someone hears..." Elawin started.

Grams snorted indelicately, making Taeva smirk and sending Leena into a fit of giggles. "What are they going to do? Lock up an old woman? Pah!" She winked at Taeva and Leena. "They'd have to catch me first! I've worked in a tavern my entire life. I'm spicy."

They stayed against the walls of the florist shop until most of the crowd had thinned out, then started making their way back to The Honey Goblet. Leena, her heavy backpack bending her beneath its weight, came with them.

"You don't have lessons?" Taeva asked.

"They're canceled for the next three days for 'honor and remembrance,'" Leena said, her voice taking on a mockingly ancient, droning quality. "But I think the Watch has pulled all the Head Wizards away from their lectures to help with the investigation."

"They should have it figured out in no time, then," Taeva said.

Leena rolled her eyes. "Hardly. We don't have any necromancers in the city. By the time one gets here, the body will be rotten, and no one will be able to speak to them anymore. Even the Head Wizards have little more to work with than the Watch."

"Oh," Taeva said, scowling at the thought of speaking to dead bodies. As useful as it no doubt was in cases like this, she was glad that responsibility wouldn't fall on her shoulders.

They turned a corner, the crowd thinning out a little more as people turned toward their homes and jobs on different streets. Leena, though, moved closer to Taeva.

"Did you see Head Watchman Wolfstone?" she whispered conspiratorially.

"No," Taeva answered.

"He looks awful. Like he hasn't slept a wink since the murders."

"There's probably a lot of pressure on him from the other nobles," Taeva answered, remembering what Grams had said.

They rounded the next bend, turning onto The Honey Goblet's street. A crowd of people had already formed out front, waiting for the Goldmeads to get home and open for the day.

Taeva let out a groan. "This is going to be a mess."

"I'll help," Leena said, hitching her bag higher on her back. "Just put me straight to work."

"I heard someone asking for work," Taeva's mother said, dropping back to walk beside them. "Don't worry, we're going to have plenty to go around!"

Chapter Five

The crowd parted to let them through, a mixture of smiling faces and scowls of impatience greeting them.

Taeva plastered her practiced grin in place, ready to fall into her all-to-familiar role, but she couldn't help but scan the crowd, searching for even a hint of a sage green cloak. She was fairly certain that she hadn't seen any of that particular green in the Grand Square anywhere other than in the Watchman's hair, but what if she was wrong? What if that first glimpse had been the edge of a cloak? It would mean the Sage Reavers were in Grandhaven. What she'd do if she found them in the crowd, she didn't know. Hide in her room, most likely.

"Give us a few, and we'll be ready for you," Tirson told the queue. He held the door open for Taeva and the others, then locked it firmly behind them again. "Alright people, let's get moving!"

Taeva threw the curtains open on the side and rear windows, leaving the front for last. She lit the candles, stoked the fire in the hearth, and went through the sitting area again, making sure they hadn't missed any messes when they locked up the night before. Leena dropped her heavy pack behind the bar, then disappeared into the kitchen with Taeva's mother and Grams. She came back out before Taeva was able to finish her final round.

"Magic," she said with a grin. "Stoves and ovens already heated for the day."

Taeva smiled back, but it felt brittle at the edges. She should be able to lend that help every day, using music to wield the required magic. Except she couldn't. She couldn't bring herself to even try.

"That's so wonderful! Especially with all the people waiting," she said. The compliment was sincere, but the words still tasted like ash. "Help me give everything one more once-over, please? Then we can open."

In record time, they were pulling aside the last of the curtains and propping the front door open. The crowd outside had grown even more as they prepared for the day, and all thoughts of music and magic were driven out of Taeva's mind as she hustled through the lunchtime rush. It was a huge help to have Leena working as an extra server. The half-elf learned their routine and, in no time, was working with Taeva to take orders at the bar and deliver food through the tables. Everything was going smoothly until a hand shot out as she passed one of the tables and grabbed Taeva's arm.

She staggered to a stop, expecting a pushy customer she would have to soothe. But it was even worse. It was her first violin teacher, Madam Tifera.

Taeva froze, her heart lodging itself in her throat. The wizened woman smiled, letting go of Taeva's arm. She thought of running and hiding in the kitchen, but her feet were stuck to the floor as surely as if roots had grown over them and tangled around her ankles.

The elderly elf looked exactly as Taeva remembered her. The same steel-grey braid hanging well past her hips. The same keen blue eyes that could spot tension in Taeva's bow hand from across a concert hall. She was even dressed the same. She always wore flowing gowns fit for solo performances, her shoulders bared. Today's dress was a deep rose, trimmed in gold, and cinched tightly at the waist. Madam Tifera folded her dexterous fingers on the table in front of her.

"How have you been, dear?" she asked.

Taeva fought for words. Madam Tifera was a brilliant musician. Over the course of her long life, she'd mastered multiple instruments. She could play circles around almost anyone on the violin, the harpsichord, the lute, even wind instruments like the flute, and, oddly enough, the bagpipes. Taeva had always been intimidated by her. It had cost her parents a small fortune to secure her lessons with such a renowned master.

"Well—" Her voice came out in a squeak, and she cleared her throat. "I've been doing well, thank you. How are you?"

"Excellent," Tifera answered. She ignored Taeva's hollow pleasantries and barreled ahead to even more awkward ground. "How are your lessons with the bard going? I was so upset to see you leave, but I understand the appeal of working magic into your playing."

Taeva's heart wedged itself in her throat. She had to fight to draw breath. There was no way she would be able to get any words out.

Leena saved her again. She appeared at Taeva's elbow with Tifera's order.

"Watered wine and the lemon fish," the wizard said brightly. "I've been hoping to catch you about your lyre, Madam Tifera. Mom had a question."

Leena pushed against Taeva, slowly shoving her away to stand in her place. She put her hands behind her back and flapped them in a shooing motion. Taeva took the hint and fled back to the bar.

What a terrible week this was shaping up to be. She'd been home for four months and hadn't dealt with this much of her past coming up in all that time. Now it was all rising to the surface like stink in a bog. She owed Leena a string of favors, not only for helping work through the rush but for saving her from all these awkward and painful conversations.

She took two more orders and delivered them, carefully avoiding going anywhere near Madam Tifera's table. It was obvious she was going out of her way to avoid the elf, but she was beyond caring.

"This has been pretty fun," Leena said. She dropped a set of dirty dishes off in the kitchen and circled back behind the bar. "Definitely better than sitting at home in the shop and listening to my mom and brother planing wood all day."

Taeva smiled—a real one this time. "About before ... thank you for distracti—"

Leena cut her off, grabbing her sleeve and staring pointedly at the door.

Tybrecht Wolfstone walked in.

Leena hadn't exaggerated at all. The Head Watchman looked awful. Granted, Wolfstone had never looked particularly great—in Taeva's opinion—any of the times he'd been in the tavern. He looked perpetually haggard and overworked. Dark circles hung permanently under his eyes, and his short salt-and-pepper hair usually looked like it was a little overdue for a cut. He was the perfect example of the type of Watchman who let themselves go in favor of their work. In contrast to his own rough edges, though, his uniform was always sharp, with crisp, well-starched creases and not a thread out of place.

But now he looked like he hadn't changed clothes in days. Pale and worn, he sauntered up to the bar to order, giving Taeva a small wave. The corners of his lips tipped up, but no emotion reached his red and watery eyes.

Taeva shared a concerned glance with Leena before moving over to take the Head Watchmen's order. "How are you today?" she asked. She regretted the words as soon as they were out of her mouth.

"Exhausted," he answered frankly with a weak chuckle. "And I might be coming down with a cold because of it. If only I had a half-orc's strength or an elf's resistance to illness. The king and the nobles have been running us all ragged with their worry that their throats will be next."

"Did the Head Wizards help uncover any new leads?" Leena asked. She leaned forward on the bar, eager for information.

Wolfstone scoffed. "No such luck. Let me get a mead, your choice, and the chef's choice on the meal. I haven't had good food or a nice drink since they woke me and rushed me to Amberwood's house. Anything will do."

He slid his coin across the bar, and Leena collected it while Taeva put his order in and poured a goblet of her favorite mead. She scooted it across the bar toward him.

"It's our best mead. It's been so popular this year that we're on our last two barrels. It's made with wildflower…"

She trailed off as Wolfstone pulled a folded paper packet out of the inside pocket of his coat. He upended it over the top of his goblet, pouring a fine teal powder into the mead.

"Got a spoon I can use?" he asked. Taeva pulled one out from the shelves under the bar and handed it to him. He stirred the power into his drink with frustrated aggression. "Hopefully the mead will hide the flavor. As common as headache medicine is, you'd think they'd have found a way to make it less bitter."

"Not likely," Leena said. "The painkillers they often use are derived from willow bark, and it's such a potent flavor it'd be nearly impossible to hide."

Wolfstone took a sip and grimaced. "Ah. You're right. Still awful."

Taeva winced in sympathy. "Grams said the Watch gets a free refill on the house, so your second one will hopefully taste better. And we'll bring your food by when it's ready."

Wolfstone took another sip, looking even more pained than the first time. "Perfect, thank you." He drifted away in search of an empty table.

"They shouldn't be pushing the Watch so hard. They're all just people, even the wizards. He looks like he's about to drop in his tracks," Taeva said.

"They wouldn't be so motivated if there hadn't been a noble involved," Grams said, coming out of the kitchen carrying two dishes. "If it was you or I, it'd be business as usual."

"Grams..." Taeva said in a tone that reminded her too much of her mother.

"What? Just saying the truth. Again."

"I'll take those, Grams," Leena said. She scooped up the food and hustled out to deliver it to the waiting customers.

"Your new friend sure is useful, sugar," Grams said, watching her go. "Never had the oven up to temperature so quickly. We might hire her, wizard or not." She spun back into the kitchen, an approving smile on her lips.

Friend? Taeva thought. Was that what Leena was?

Taeva had always had friends *before*. Musicians and

bards liked to keep together, even those who played different instruments, because they had so much in common—not to mention the opportunities to collaborate. She'd left her friends behind, though, when she left Grandhaven. She hadn't had the courage to look them back up since she'd returned. Would they even still want to be friends with her if she couldn't share music and magic with them anymore?

It was especially painful that she wasn't sure what the answer would be.

I really hope Leena is a friend, she thought, watching the wizard help another table of patrons. She sure needed one.

Chapter
Six

The surge of customers following the funeral ceremony carried well into the evening until Tirson had to shoo the last few stragglers away, a tired but genuine smile on his face. The following day, unfortunately, was quiet by comparison. Lunch time had been busy enough to keep Taeva distracted, but as the afternoon dragged on, their customers drifted away and left the tavern empty.

It happened so rarely it was almost cause for panic. Even more so with the morose way Taeva's mind was prone to wandering.

So she threw herself into cleaning. She polished the bar top and the tables until they gleamed. She fetched more candles from the closet upstairs and replaced the ones that had burned down the night before. She was dusting the paintings that hung on the stone walls—oil paintings of bees and local flowers, done by her great-grandfather—when Leena walked in.

"It's already shining in here, Taeva. You should take a break," she said. She was wrapped in her uniform robes, even though the Academy was still closed while the Head Wizards worked with the Watch.

Taeva loathed the idea of getting caught sitting idly behind the bar. It's not that she would get in any kind of trouble, it's just that her father would take the opportunity to pull her into another lecture on properly aging and clearing the lees out of mead. The very idea of it made her head ache. But she answered with a simple, "Trying to stay busy," in her most cheerful, customer-facing voice.

Leena lifted a brow at her, and Taeva knew she hadn't fooled the wizard. "Well, since you're doing busy work, I have a better idea. All the other students at the Academy have been talking about this new troop of street performers. They can't shut up about them." She rolled her eyes dramatically. "The troop is performing in the Grand Square today, so I thought I'd go see what all the fuss is about. For research. Do you want to come with me?"

Troop. Performing. *Music.*

Leena hadn't said it outright, but Taeva would bet all her coin that anyone performing, especially in an area like the Grand Square, would have musical accompaniment of some kind. The beginnings of panic fluttered in the pit of her stomach.

"I can't leave right now. It's... I mean, we could get really busy at any moment," she finished, looking around the tavern and hoping another excuse would present itself.

Leena's other brow lifted to join the first. She glanced at the empty hall, making a show of searching for a customer. "I think they can spare you."

"I... But..." Taeva stammered.

The problem was she did want to go. She wanted to get out of the tavern and into the crisp autumn air, but she didn't want to go see musicians. And she couldn't think of any other excuse.

Leena's expression softened. "Look. I've noticed how panicked you get when someone mentions music and how you used to play." Taeva's heart slammed against her ribs, but Leena continued in a gentle tone. "Like that, actually.

But you can't want to keep feeling like that. Right? Maybe if you're around it for a little bit at a time, it'll get less scary. We'll go listen, see what the fuss is about, and if it's making you entirely miserable, we'll leave. Quickly and easily. We won't be trapped out there."

Taeva paused, willing herself to breathe at a steady, even rate. Somehow, the distinction between being able to flee and being stuck in the middle of it while working made more of a difference than she would have expected. It was such a small thing, but maybe she would be able to enjoy listening to a few tunes. And that would be lovely. She could admit to herself, even if she refused to say it out loud, that she missed it.

But what if the performers were people she knew? People she'd played with before she left? She'd be so embarrassed.

"I'm not sure," she said, unable to meet Leena's gaze. She'd run out of excuses unless she was going to come clean. And *that* she couldn't bear the thought of.

"I won't hear another word of it!" Grams shouted. She stormed out of the kitchen, throwing a cloth over her shoulder, her wild grey hair billowing around her like a storm cloud. "Sugar. Go with your friend. We're deader than Lord Amberwood today. Go have some fun."

Leena laughed while Taeva stared at her grandmother, gobsmacked. "You heard the lady! Let's go," the wizard said.

She grabbed Taeva by the arm and all but dragged her through the front door.

TAEVA STILL HAD ON HER APRON—SHE WASN'T GIVEN THE chance to take it off before being pulled away—and she worried at its front pocket as she followed Leena through the city.

"If these performers aren't as good as everyone has made them sound, I'm going to be so annoyed," Leena said.

They passed by a bakery, the scent of cinnamon and sugar wafting through the front door. Taeva normally would have been tempted to duck inside and buy a pastry, but her stomach was in so many knots it was likely to come back up again.

"Are they new to the city?" she asked, trying to school her voice into calmness but still warbling over the last syllable. Was it too much to ask that they be no one she'd heard of and, even more importantly, people who had never heard of her?

"No, but they're new to working together. From what I've heard, anyway." Leena glanced at Taeva, her expression guarded.

The flickering panic in Taeva's stomach swelled into a swarm of angry bees, buzzing and bouncing around. She fought the urge to turn and run all the way back to her room.

"Almost there," Leena said, as if she could sense Taeva's growing unease. "We'll give it a try, and we can leave whenever you want."

Taeva nodded, hands still picking her pocket apart. Leena looped an arm through hers and dragged her forward at a near-trot.

The Grand Square bustled with people. Nobles and well-to-do merchants went in and out of the expensive shops lining the courtyard, their many pieces of jewelry and richly dyed silks flashing in the bright autumn sunlight.

And within the Square itself, a miniature city of wood and canvas stood. King Dragonsbane allowed a certain number of vendors to set up in the Square itself, selected by a lottery. After the funeral, vendor booths had grown up like a well-organized garden to form a secondary set of streets through the Square. Anything and everything was for sale, and usually at fair and competitive prices.

Like the merchants, only a certain number of performers were allowed to showcase their skills in the square each day. There could be one in each corner and no more. It kept them from competing too closely with each other and trying to play over one another. If that happened, it would stop being music and just be noise. And noise was bad for business—no one wanted to hang around and listen to two bands trying to out-play each other.

"Do you know which corner they're playing in?" Taeva asked. They walked past a leatherworker displaying cases meant for carrying scrolls. Taeva thought of the leather case propped in the corner of her room and snatched her gaze away.

"I do. Everyone kept talking about it, you know," Leena answered, waving her hand. But she couldn't wave away Taeva's unease.

The wizard led the way, her eyes straight ahead, not sparing even a single glance for any of the wares on display. It wasn't long before Taeva heard the first few notes of music carrying over the noise of the crowd. Her anxiety sent a jolt of electricity down her spine, but she focused on her breathing and willed herself forward. She might not be one of the heroes from her novels, but she was certainly brave enough to face some music in a public square. Or at least that's what she told herself.

As they got closer to the northeastern corner of the square, she could tell the music came from a lute, a flute, and some kind of drum like what the performers had at The

Honey Goblet a few days ago. She heard none of the bright notes that came from a violin. It was more of a relief than it should have been, and though that would have embarrassed her to admit out loud, her steps felt lighter all the same.

Leena parted the crowd as they worked their way to the front. At one point, a bear of a man with pale blond hair stood with his back toward them in the middle of two stalls, oblivious that anyone would want to pass through. When he didn't respond to Leena's polite "excuse me," she smirked at Taeva and muttered a spell under her breath. The tips of her fingers glowed bright orange, and she pressed them to the man's upper arm.

"Ack!" he yelled, jumping like he'd been stung. "Blighted wasps! Watch yerselves, ladies."

He shuffled out of their way, glaring at the air over their heads, looking for his phantom wasps. Taeva and Leena nearly choked on their laughter as they hurried to vanish back into the crowd.

All too soon, however, Leena elbowed her way between a pair of half-orcs and a human in the purple and silver uniform of the royal palace. Just like that, they were at the front of the crowd, the performers a mere handful of paces away. Taeva's mouth fell open. She'd been able to hear snatches of the playing as they walked up, growing louder and clearer the closer they got, and she'd known they were good. She wasn't ready for how good.

The flutist was a bard. A tall, elegant elf with pale skin and sleek, dark hair, she swayed as gracefully as a willow in the wind as she played. Ribbons of green, teal, and purple light wound around her, then drifted through the air to coil around the limbs of an acrobat as she flipped, pirouetted, and twirled with the music—a reel, in joyful E major. They were dressed all in grey, the drab uniforms working to highlight the glow of the magic. A lutist sat on a stool, playing clear and ringing chords in a steady, flawless rhythm. His shaggy brown hair stuck out from under his grey cap and hung into his eyes, but he didn't look like he needed to watch the frets on his lute at all. The drum Taeva had heard was his doing, too. He kicked at a drum on the ground, holding a steady beat.

Taeva stood there, mouth still dangling open, until the tune finished and the crowd broke into applause. She jumped and joined in, clapping so hard her palms stung, until the next tune began.

She'd never seen magic used with music like that, even while she was studying it. Her master had stressed its value, taught her complex spells for healing and combat, but never for enjoyment. For entertainment. A thought crept up from the back of her mind: maybe she would be better at this kind of magic. She stamped it down before she could get carried away. It would be too dangerous. She couldn't trust her magic after what had happened. She'd only ever had tentative control of it. It would be too easy to get distracted in a place like this, and that could be disastrous.

And that meant she couldn't trust her music, either. The magic always rose to meet it too easily.

The crowd clapped as the tune came to an end, and Taeva joined in half-heartedly. She wanted to be polite—the music had been excellent—but her earlier enthusiasm had run dry.

At least I didn't run away, she thought wryly.

"We're going to take a short break, everyone, but don't go far! We've got lots more to play," the lutist announced in a clear, deep voice. People tossed coins into his open lute case, and he thanked them, sweeping into a graceful bow.

Now that the playing and the show were finished,

Taeva's nerves started up again. The more she looked at the elven flutist, the more familiar the bard looked. "I think I want to lea—"

"Kellan!" Leena cut her off, waving to the lutist. His smile brightened, and he started walking towards them.

Taeva forgot about her nerves again. "You know him?" she hissed, grabbing Leena's sleeve.

"I might have lied a little." The wizard had the good grace to look ashamed. Barely. "It's true I hadn't seen them play, though."

"Overhollow," the lutist said as he drew up to them. "You'll have to thank your mother for me. The adjustments she made to my lute were perfect. The action is so light now."

"Of course. Kellan, this is my friend, Taeva Goldmead. Taeva, this is Kellan Cliffrose, prodigious lutist and unashamed pain in my ass."

Kellan rolled his eyes, but they twinkled with mirth as he turned to Taeva, offering his hand. He looked to be about Taeva's age—maybe a few years older. His smile lit up his warm brown eyes. The beginnings of a beard covered his strong jaw, and instead of making him look sloppy, it made him look roguish. Like he was secretly dangerous.

So handsome, Taeva thought like an awestruck fool as she took his hand. His callouses from plucking the strings scratched across her palm in a way that shouldn't have been so delightful.

"Your playing was wonderful. I haven't seen someone play two instruments like that before," she managed to stammer out. "And whoever transposed the fiddle part of that reel for the lute did an excellent job."

Kellan paused, his hand still holding hers. Surprise flitted across his features but was quickly replaced by an even broader smile. "Thank you! I did it." He noticed he still held her hand and pulled it away, pressing his palm to the side of his leg. "A fellow musician, I take it? Or a bard?"

Taeva's stomach flipped, but Leena answered with a quick half-lie. "You'd be surprised what all you pick up when you grow up in a tavern as popular as The Honey Goblet." Taeva breathed a sigh of relief. Leena had come to her rescue again. She owed the half-elf so many favors—and an extra large one in this case.

"I love that tavern," Kellan said. "Haven't been by in a while, though. I'll have to stop in soon."

"You should," Taeva said, caught somewhere between a rote response to encourage business and genuinely hoping to see him again. "I should get back before the dinner rush, though." She took Leena's shoulders and turned her back the way they'd come, allowing for no argument. "Lyria grant you no broken strings," she called over her shoulder, then cursed under her breath. She'd never heard someone who wasn't a musician invoke the goddess of song.

They'd worked their way back into the press when they heard Kellan call for them. "Wait!" The crowd parted for him to come through, as easily as calm water around the bow of a ship. He held two envelopes out for them, one in each hand, sealed in bright blue wax. "I'm playing at a ball at Lord Silversage's place in two days. I have some extra tickets if you'd like to come."

Leena's eyes lit up. "Is there free food?"

Kellan laughed. "And drink. All the fancy stuff."

"We'll be there," Leena answered before Taeva could think of an excuse. She snatched both the invitations away from Kellan and shoved Taeva's into her hands.

Then Kellan's gaze met her, the faintest rose-colored blush spreading across his cheeks before he jogged back to his place with his lute. Taeva could feel her own blush burning on her cheeks.

"I guess I'm going to a ball," she whispered.

LATER THAT NIGHT AS TAEVA GOT READY FOR BED, SHE WAS still thinking about Kellan and his band of performers.

She sat on the edge of her bed in her nightgown, finger-combing her hair and turning it into an even bigger blonde poof. She'd lit a single candle, and it burned down on her battered desk beneath her window. Moths hurled themselves at the glass, trying to get to the light. Shadows danced over her wardrobe, her bookshelf, and the empty music stand wedged between them. The down of her mattress smushed around her and beckoned her in, but her mind was spinning too fast to go to sleep just yet. Besides, every time she closed her eyes she saw the bard's whirls of magical light curling behind her eyelids. She couldn't keep herself from thinking about what might have been.

What if she'd worked with that kind of magic instead of more dangerous, nerve-wracking spells? Would she have ever left? Would the accident have been avoided entirely?

She picked at a loose thread on her quilt, her eyes sliding past her overstuffed bookshelf, packed full of novels about adventure and magic. She'd spent so long lost in those stories and other worlds, wishing she was a hero. She scoffed. *Look how that turned out.* She pulled her eyes away, only for her gaze to land on the leather case propped up in the corner.

Her violin. It hadn't moved from that spot since she'd returned home. She tried her best not to even look at it. But she could pick it up now. She could put a heavy practice mute on it to keep from disturbing her family. She could tune it, could play a few scales. She might even be able to summon her own dancing ribbons of light.

No.

She slammed the door on those thoughts and blew out her candle. Curling up under her warm blankets, she squeezed her eyes shut and willed herself to think of something—anything—but the flutist bard and her glimmering magic.

Chapter Seven

"What do you think?" Taeva's father asked expectantly. "Don't taste it yet; just look at the color. Swirl it around. Smell it."

Taeva started at the mead in the tasting glass, trying to glean some kind of answer from the golden liquid. Her family stood around her, waiting. To her, it was more pressure than playing in a crowded concert hall used to be.

She sniffed at the drink, getting a light hint of the pumpkin and cinnamon her father worked into the autumn mead. "It doesn't smell bitter."

Tirson's hopeful expression curdled. "And? Do you think it's ready?"

Taeva sighed, already certain she was about to get another lecture. "I'd have to taste it," she answered. Defeated, she passed the glass back to Tirson, who sat it on the bar beside them.

"Taeva, honey, how long have we been doing this?" he asked.

She fought back a groan. "Three generations."

"Right. And you'll be the fourth. You should know the mead better than this by now."

"Tirson, don't you talk to her like that," Grams piped in. "She's not a younger version of you. She's got to sort it out for herself. She'll get the hang of it."

"And the records..." Taeva's mother started.

"No one can read that blasted scrawl! Clean it up, and I'm sure she'd have the books and the recipes figured out in no time, like what I've been doing with the recipes for the food."

Taeva stayed quiet and traced the grains of the wood on the bar as they argued about her. Again. She was grateful to her grandmother for coming to her defense, but it couldn't be missed that she also assumed Taeva would take over the tavern. The only difference was she wanted to let Taeva figure that out for herself instead of strong-arming her into it. At least that's how it felt to Taeva.

But the end result was still the same. Stifling pressure.

"Taeva! Are you ready?" Leena's voice cut through the argument before she even passed through the threshold, robes billowing behind her once again. She'd come close to shouting, like she'd heard the altercation happening and was determined to cut it to the quick.

"Ready?" Tirson asked, brow creasing. "Are you going somewhere, Taeva?"

Taeva had no idea. She looked to Leena with pleading eyes.

"Dress shopping," Leena answered brightly. "We're going to a ball tomorrow night."

"A ball!" Elawin exclaimed, delighted. "How did you get tickets?"

"Wizarding secret," Leena said. "But I need a dress, and I need Taeva's help picking one out."

Taeva needed a dress, too. She hadn't even thought that far ahead. She'd been too overwhelmed by the events of the day to have started preparing.

"She was gone part of the day yesterday, too," Tirson protested.

"Don't you dare," Grams started.

"She has to go—she doesn't have anything to wear to a ball," Elawin added. "We've run things without her before, so one more afternoon won't hurt. It's a *ball*, darling. And she's a guest! Not a caterer."

"Out you go," Grams said, once more shuffling them toward the door before Taeva's father could protest any further. She pressed a coin purse into Taeva's hands. "Nope, no arguments! Go get something pretty."

Chastised, Taeva paused only long enough to untie her apron and plop in onto the bar. It felt like a tiny act of rebellion, and her heart hammered in her chest as she chased Leena out into the street.

WITH THE DIRECT MANNER THAT TAEVA HAD COME TO EXPECT from the wizard, Leena led them to a dress shop two blocks from the Grand Square. Taeva followed behind her, nervously weighing her coin pouches. The shops in that part of the city catered to all the nobles that lived around the palace and the Grand Square. They were known for being expensive. She didn't think either of them had the coin for the kind of shops the nobles frequented. Nor did they have the time for custom work at more modest stores. She hoped they'd be able to find dresses that fit well enough that they wouldn't need alterations. And that Leena wasn't taking them somewhere where they'd be too out of place.

When she expressed her concern to her friend, Leena only brushed her off, saying, "The Final Stitches will have something. They always do."

When they arrived at the shop, Taeva was surprised by the size of it. Easily twice the size of the neighboring stores, the rippling glass of the oversized front windows showed walls and racks full of dresses in every color imaginable. The round sign over the front door was carved with a spool of thread and a needle, both painted in shining silver. A bell jangled over the door as they walked inside.

Before Taeva could even draw a breath, a seamstress was at her elbow, a measuring tape slung around her spindly neck and a tiny pin cushion loaded with pins and needles strapped to her wrist. A pencil held her steel grey bun in a messy knot on the very top of her head.

"With that glorious hair and your fair complexion, you shouldn't be wearing such dark tones," she said, eyeing Taeva's navy-and-white skirt and bodice combination. "You're a spring, maybe an autumn. Definitely not a winter."

Taeva took a step back, unsure how to respond. But the woman wasn't done.

She rounded on Leena. "And you. The Academy has such unflattering robes. I don't know what event you're shopping for today, but it hardly matters. Whatever it is, *those* simply will not do."

Taeva realized her mouth was hanging open for the second time in two days. She closed it with a snap. She'd never felt so attacked for just walking through a door.

"We'll keep that in mind while we browse," Leena said, matching the woman's imperious tone. "We won't need anything altered, but if we need help, we'll let you know."

The seamstress gave her a respectful nod, then whirled and stormed away, returning to a mannequin in the rear corner where she was draping a rich crimson silk.

"I've been in here a few times with Mother," Leena whispered, leaning towards Taeva. "She's the fastest seamstress in the city, but she isn't the easiest to deal with. Geniuses and eccentricities and all."

"I'm glad you knew how to handle her," Taeva said as

she looked around the shop, already slightly overwhelmed by the choices.

"Let's start ... here," Leena said, picking a rack at random and sliding dresses around.

Leena skipped around the shop, flittering from a rack to the hangers on the wall to a different rack whenever a color or texture caught her eye. Taeva worked more methodically, mapping the place out in her mind and moving through it in a vaguely linear way, worried she would miss something. Eventually, their paths crossed again, and Leena paused, a sapphire and silver gown draped over her arm.

"Do your parents always pressure you about the tavern like that?" she asked without warning.

Taeva froze, her hand on a sage green gown with rose trim. She thought about lying to Leena—or at least lying by omission—so she didn't have to dredge up anything painful or awkward, but it made her feel dirty. She didn't deserve to call Leena her friend if she lied to her face when she was obviously trying to help. She owed her the truth. It was too difficult to look at Leena while she spoke, but she would try to be open and honest.

"They do, yes. It's been a bit worse since I came back home a few months ago, though," she said. That old feeling of failure and regret surged up, and she pushed the green dress away. She'd been wearing green when the incident occurred. She still couldn't bring herself to wear it again.

"Where had you gone?" Leena asked. She kept shuffling dresses around, interested and listening, but not focused solely on Taeva. It helped.

"Not far," Taeva admitted. "Only one city away. To Brineport."

"For bard work?"

Taeva winced. Leena's ability to suss out the truth was

going to make her an impressive and powerful wizard one day. Right then, though, it was terribly inconvenient. Taeva took a deep breath and confessed. "It was. It ... didn't go well."

"Mmm," Leena held up a plum dress, then shook her head and placed it back on the rack. "Not everything goes perfectly the first time we try it. Sometimes it doesn't work right the first ten or twenty times. In that regard, life and magic are very much alike."

Taeva turned to face her, brow furrowed in thought. "I suppose you're right."

"Of course I am," Leena said with a teasing grin. "And if you want to talk about it more, I'll be glad to listen and offer more wisdom. Here's more right now. This is your dress."

She pulled a gown off the rack with a flourish. It was as black as night, with stars embroidered on the bodice in gold and silver thread. Each star was tiny, picked out in painstaking detail. Taeva even saw familiar constellations embroidered into the silk. The sleeves were sheer, definitely more for looks than to be warm, and floated like mist. The skirt had several splits, revealing a shimmering gold and silver underskirt that flashed like a meteor shower.

It was gorgeous, and Taeva wanted it the moment she set eyes on it. "But the seamstress said I should avoid dark colors."

Leena rolled her eyes. "Everyone looks good in black. Go try it on."

HER COIN PURSES SIGNIFICANTLY LIGHTER IN HER POCKET, Taeva walked with Leena back to The Honey Goblet, the night dress clutched to her chest. It was a little too small, but the corseted back meant she could let it out enough to comfortably wear, so it was perfect as far as she was concerned.

"I've never spent so much on a dress before," Taeva said. "But I don't regret it."

"Goddesses, no. That thing is perfect. Kellan is going to love it," Leena replied, smirking yet again.

"Kellan? We just met!" Taeva blushed. It would have been a lie to say she hadn't considered his opinion when she'd tried it on. Not that it should matter; they didn't know each other.

Leena rolled her eyes dramatically, and Taeva cocked her head, thinking she must have missed something.

"He invited *you*. I just happened to have been there. He didn't want to look rude," Taeva argued.

Leena snorted. "He's never invited me to anything. I've known him for years, but only from the shop. He couldn't take his eyes off you. I was the one who got invited by chance."

"Oh," was all Taeva could say in reply. Surely Leena had misread the situation. It was too much to hope that he'd specifically wanted her to go. It had to have been a happy coincidence.

Her imagination ran with the idea, though, conjuring up an image of her and Kellan twirling across a gleaming marble floor, her dress fanning out around her. She reined herself in with a frown. There was no sense in indulging in such fantasies. If he found out that she used to play, and about the disaster she'd caused, any interest Leena thought he had would shrivel up and die.

No, it was better not to let herself even begin to hope.

They turned off The Final Stitches's street and fell in behind a couple of Watchmen. The pair of human men walked side-by-side, heads turning every which way as they scanned the foot traffic. Both of their uniforms were rumpled like they'd been wearing them all day and then some.

"What a farce," the tall one complained. "We're only out here to look like we're accomplishing something. No amount of walking around is going to produce the killer."

Taeva and Leena glanced at each other, then walked a little faster, trying to get close enough to hear the shorter guard's reply.

"...get paid, I'll walk all they want. Got mouths to feed."

"But we could be doing something useful. You know what they say about Amberwood. Killer's long dead by now. Probably rotting in some hole in the slums."

"No, I don't know what they say about him," the shorter guard grumbled. "I'm too busy working to keep up with gossip."

His partner ignored the slight. "He kept his blade poisoned. Real deadly. So if he got a cut up like Wolfstone thinks, the murder's already dead." He spit in the gutter. "Better death than he deserved, most like."

Taeva and Leena turned off the street, leaving the guards and their gossip behind.

"I didn't know people actually kept poison on their blades," Leena said after the guards were out of earshot. "That's like something out of an adventure novel."

"It is," Taeva agreed. "But if the murderer really was poisoned and is already gone, that's a relief."

It honestly felt a little anticlimactic to her, but that was kind of thing you kept to yourself. Real life wasn't as exciting as her novels. Quick justice was much better than a long, drawn out investigation that might not ever be completed.

"Hopefully it's enough for them to let the guards get

some rest. And the Head Wizards too." They stopped outside of The Honey Goblet, and Leena pulled her own dress closer to her chest. "Can I come by early tomorrow to get ready?"

Taeva beamed. "Of course!"

Leena smiled back, every bit as bright. "Perfect! See you then!" She skipped gracefully down the street, headed home to Overhollow Fine Instruments.

Taeva went straight up to her room and hung her new dress on the edge of her bookshelf. It struck her that she was very much looking forward to the next day. She hadn't felt that way in a long time, and it warmed her from her chest out, all the way to her toes. She dared to look at the mournful violin case in the corner and hummed a triumphant tune to herself. Not even that could bring her down.

Chapter Eight

*L*eena swept through the front doors in the middle of the lunchtime rush, her ballgown tossed over one shoulder, streaming out behind her, and her usual pack over the other. She snatched Taeva up in her wake, and they disappeared upstairs to get ready, Tirson scowling after them while Grams and Elawin smiled and waved them away.

They sequestered themselves in Taeva's room. Leena dumped her bag on the bed, and pins, brushes, and all manner of cosmetics spilled out.

"You first," the half-elf commanded. "Sit." She pointed at the edge of the bed while she dug around in her bag.

Taeva obliged, folding her hands in her lap. "Have you ever been to a ball before?"

Leena attacked her hair with a comb and a determined expression. "No, have you?"

Taeva hesitated, but only for a heartbeat. "I played at one once, as part of a full orchestra. The hall was decorated with thousands of flowers. It must have cost a fortune."

Leena curled a lock of Taeva's hair up onto the crown of her head. "You should tell Kellan you play violin. He'd love that."

Taeva cringed at the very idea. "Used to play," she corrected. "There's no sense in telling him about something I don't do anymore."

Leena paused to study her. "If you say so," she finally answered. "I think we should leave some of your hair down. What do you think?"

Two hours later, they were ready. They'd both lined their eyes in kohl and carefully painted their lips in carmine. Leena wore her hair pinned up on the sides, and it fell in dark waves down past her waist. She'd also helped Taeva pin her mass of blonde curls up, leaving a few strategic pieces loose to frame her face. When she looked at her reflection in the hall mirror on their way out, Taeva barely recognized herself.

"We look like twilight and the night," she muttered, standing next to Leena in her dark sapphire gown.

Leena tilted her head, studying their reflection. "Lyria, goddess of song, and Losharva, goddess of magic, descended to the mortal realm to grace the Silversage ball with our presence."

Taeva chortled and elbowed Leena in the ribs, but the playful fantasy buoyed her. She left like she was floating the entire walk to the Grand Square.

The Silversage mansion was one of the largest around the Square. Lord Mikriel Silversage was considered *new money* by all the old noble families. He hadn't been born into obscene wealth but rather had invested and plotted—some said conned—his way into vast stores of gold. Then he'd swooped in on the late widow, Lady Glassing, and purchased her home before she was even in the crypt. It'd been all the city could talk about for years. Thus, he'd set himself up directly across from the palace, like he needed to keep his next target lined up.

It was well known that the nobility hated him, but no one turned down an invitation to one of his parties. He was just too rich to ignore, Taeva supposed. And from the way people were lined up outside of the Silversage house, light from the stained glass windows spilling out over the street and over the waiting guests, he'd sent out a lot of invitations and not a single one had been turned down.

When Taeva and Leena got up to the door, a pair of half-orc guards stopped them and, without a word, held out their hands for invitations. The girls handed them over, then watched as the guards scrutinized them with furious scowls. Taeva smoothed out her skirt and straightened her spine, trying to mimic the posture of the noble women in line. Finally, the guards nodded and waved them forward. Taeva glanced at Leena, who waggled her brows and marched ahead, unruffled.

As soon as they stepped through the front doors, an usher appeared beside them. He was a human, dressed in a black coat and trousers, a stiff, heavily-starched collar brushing the edge of his jaw. "Right this way, ladies. I'll take you to the ballroom."

Taeva looked at Leena again and mouthed, *Is this normal?*

Leena shrugged as they crossed into the entrance hall.

Marble floors, polished to a high shine, clicked under their heels. Doors, themselves intricately carved and meticulously clean, lined either side of the hall, all shut fast. Staircases swept up to their left and right, carpeted in deep scarlet, both ending on a balcony with a gold and white railing. A set of tall double doors was open at the center of the balcony. The usher led them to the left set of stairs, and as they reached the halfway point, voices and the first strains of music reached them. Nerves and excitement tangled in Taeva's belly.

A tall elven couple in matching hunter green suits were

being led up the stairs in front of them, another usher walking with them.

The one on the left leaned over and said in a feigned whisper, "Can you believe he's still having this ball? After what happened only a week ago."

His date shook his head and pulled the other elf closer. "Not so loud, dear."

The first speaker scoffed. "I'm not shouting it in the middle of the dance floor. It's fine."

Taeva's brow creased. It *was* odd timing for a grand party. Half the city and all the nobility were in mourning and fearful that another attack could come at any moment. People who had been close to Lord Amberwood were probably offended that the ball hadn't been canceled. But maybe Silversage was the only one who wasn't afraid. Or maybe he just wanted to exert some sense of normalcy in his life.

The usher stopped and bowed when they reached the doors. "Please enjoy the ball." He swept away without giving them a second glance.

Then they were through the doors, and a wealth of sound and light washed over them, carrying Taeva's previous musings away like smoke in the wind.

The ballroom was massive, with tall ceilings hung with huge and elaborate chandeliers. Silversage had hired a wizard for the event because, instead of lighting the candles in the chandeliers, magical lights floated among them and danced between the carved beams in the vaulted ceiling. Buffets lined the walls on either side, laden with all manner of food and drink. People milled around, piling food onto silver dishes, and stood around cocktail tables, talking and laughing. In the center of it all, guests danced in bright twirls of silk and lace.

The glitter of it all, the way it seemed to have been pulled from a dream, stopped Taeva in her tracks. She'd played at fancy venues, been on stage before some of the very people in this room, but working at an event and attending one changed the feel entirely. The grandeur of it swept over her like the music carrying over the crowds from the far side of the ballroom.

As if on cue, the dancers reached a part in the music where they lined up across from their partners, and Taeva had a direct view of the stage and the musicians on it.

A harpsichord sat in the center of the stage, a careworn dwarf at the keys. An elf played a violin to one side of the harpsichord. Taeva's heart ached hearing the crystal clarity of the notes she played. She simultaneously wanted to stand right next to the stage to watch more closely and to flee back into the hall and weep. Then she saw Kellan. Her heart jumped up and wedged itself firmly inside her windpipe.

He sat on a stool again, lute propped in his lap and one leg extended to the floor. He looked simultaneously rakish and sophisticated with his black coattails and his hair still in disarray. As she watched, the violin and harpsichord fell silent, and Kellan flew into a solo. His fingers danced through chords, harmonics, and individual notes so pure the air almost shimmered. His playing in the Square was excellent, but now Taeva understood why Leena had called him prodigious.

It was lovely. And it made it all the more clear that he would never be interested in a washed-up bard. He was too talented to ruin his reputation with someone who couldn't even bear to touch her instrument anymore.

Leena grabbed her arm, jarring Taeva back to the present. "Close your mouth and get out of the door, friend,"

Leena said with a laugh, pulling her towards the refreshments.

Taeva did as her friend said, a furious blush burning across her cheeks. She followed Leena and prayed to all the goddesses that Kellan hadn't noticed her standing in the doorway like an idiot.

"Look at this spread!" Leena exclaimed when they got to the buffet.

Silver and crystal dishes covered every inch of the long tables. There were fruits of every kind—some clearly imported from other regions. Towers of cheeses, all neatly cut into tiny, perfect cubes. Tiny sandwiches, with or without crust. Whole entrees shrunk down into bite-sized pieces, complete with garnish—pork with tiny bits of pineapple, beef with a dollop of horseradish sauce, and a sprig of parsley. Drinks were next in line—any kind a guest could ever ask for. Sparkling white and red wines, fizzing in tall flutes. Deep red wines in glasses that looked more like bowls. Colorful cocktails with fruit hanging from the rims of the glasses. Mead and ale and liquors aplenty.

"Looks like there's enough dessert on the other side of the room to feed the entire city," Leena said, already grabbing a dish and piling food onto it. "I can't wait."

Taeva followed suit. After they'd loaded their plates and were each holding a glittering purple cocktail that neither of them could identify—it burst on Taeva's tongue with the sour-sweetness of a blackberry, then burned on the way down—they wandered to an open cocktail table. They lingered there, eating the delicious food and watching the dancers. Well, Leena watched the dancers. Taeva couldn't pull her eyes away from the stage.

"Are you alright, or is it too much?" Leena asked.

Taeva took a sip of her drink, buying herself a moment to think. Every time the violin soared above the other two instruments, or when she caught a particularly beautiful bit of vibrato, it made her chest ache. But it felt more like longing than panic. Maybe Leena was right. She just needed to be around it again.

"I am," she answered finally. "This is wonderful."

"It is, isn't it?" Leena answered before taking one final bite. Her plate, once stacked full, was miraculously empty. "Let's get dessert!"

They were at the end of the dessert tables closest to the stage, both already carrying obscene amounts of pastries, when the musicians stopped for a break. To Taeva's delight and horror, Kellan sat his lute on a stand behind his stool and made for where they stood, a broad smile on his face.

Even his teeth are pretty, she thought before mentally scolding herself. She couldn't think like that. What would someone with that much skill want with a failed bard? The thought sobered her as he walked over, easing the blush that had threatened to blaze across her face again.

He rolled his wrists and flexed his fingers, then stopped in front of them. "Been playing for over an hour," he complained, still smiling as he undid the top button on his collar. "And still more to go. My fingers might fall off."

Leena snorted. "As if you aren't used to it."

"Not at all. Not now, anyway. I rarely play at events like this anymore. It's great, don't get me wrong, but I'd rather be in a little tavern somewhere or in the Square."

"All your talent is wasted on you," Leena said, her mouth full of cheesecake.

"Goddesses, Leena!" Taeva hissed. "She didn't mean that."

"Yes, I did."

Kellan laughed. "It's fine. She's mean to me every time I go to her parents' shop." He paused and swallowed, his eyes skating over Taeva from her dress to her hair. "Are you enjoying yourself?"

She wished she hadn't noticed his gaze. That damning blush crept back into her cheeks, and words didn't seem to be able to form on her tongue.

"He got what he had coming," a deep voice said, cutting through their group and sparing Taeva from having to respond.

A half-orc dressed in impossibly fine clothes walked along the table, perusing the desserts. The burgundy wool of his jacket complimented the pale green of his skin perfectly and was clearly tailored to fit his broad frame with an exacting hand. Dark hair curled back from a strong face with no visible tusks—odd for a half-orc.

"Silversage," Leena whispered in Taeva's ear. Their host.

"You don't mean that, my lord," a gnome said from beside him. He didn't even reach Silversage's elbows. He was dressed like the usher that had led them inside, and from the way he trailed after Silversage, Taeva assumed he was the lord's steward.

"I mean every word. I'm glad Amberwood is dead," Silversage continued, his deep bass rumbling with annoyance. "Trying to buy out the Watch. Bah! And the king was considering it, too. He needed to go."

He turned from the table, dark eyes landing on Taeva and the others. They were all looking right at him, obviously listening to his every word. A scowl marred his features before he reined it in, replacing it with a more neutral expression. "Palfrey, go check on my wife," he said, waving his steward off. Then he turned back to Taeva and her friends and said, "I hope you're enjoying the party." With a tight nod, he disappeared back into the crowd.

Taeva exchanged nervous glances with Leena and Kellan.

What did we just hear?

Chapter Nine

*T*he ball whisked by in a blur of jewel-toned colors. Kellan was called back up to the stage, leaving Taeva and Leena with their desserts. Taeva chewed hers joylessly, any flavor it might have had no longer registering. She had the sickening feeling that they were eating in the home of a murderer. Or an employer of murderers. Either way, she was ready to leave but also too scared to flee. The glare Silversage had leveled at them said it all. He knew they'd heard him, at least partially. All that was left to be seen was what he would do about it.

What if we're next? she thought as she walked with Leena out of the front doors. The other guests spilled out around them, a rainbow of gowns and fine suits fanning out into the night.

"Taeva! Leena! Wait!"

They both turned to see Kellan jogging down the steps after them, his lute case bouncing against his back in a way that made Taeva cringe. The poor instrument.

Pale green caught Taeva's eye, and her heart lurched. The color was haunting her. This time it was Lord Silversage. He stood his front steps, bidding his guests farewell. He waved politely to a group of people behind her, and then his focus landed on Taeva and her friends. He gave them the same polite nod and wave, like nothing was amiss.

Maybe we don't need to worry after all. It seemed too good to be true after hearing how pleased he was about Amber-wood's murder.

"Where are the two of you headed?" Kellan asked, fighting to catch his breath.

"The Honey Goblet," Leena answered.

"I see." Kellan paused, and the short silence behind his words was painfully awkward.

"Do you want to come with us?" Taeva asked. She was proud of how normal her voice sounded. That knot was back in her throat, and she had to force out every word.

Kellan, by contrast, melted a little, tension Taeva hadn't noticed before easing from his shoulders. "I'd love to." He hitched his case up a little higher on his back, then waved them ahead. "Lead the way, ladies."

The walk back felt twice as long as the trip to the party. Leena talked most of the way, giving a running review of everything she'd eaten in the kind of detail only a wizard was capable of. Taeva and Kellan were only required to comment when she posed a question, which was rare, and even then she only wanted a one-word answer.

It was a relief. Taeva needed all of her energy just to look normal. To not walk as stiffly as a stone golem. To not stare at Kellan. She partially failed at the latter. She didn't stare, but she did steal a few glances his way. One of those times, she swore he'd been looking at her, then swiftly looked away when she turned to him. She could have been imaging it—she was surely imagining it—but it still made her blush deliriously.

Kellan and Leena followed her into The Honey Goblet not long after. The tavern had settled into its steady evening rhythm since the dinner crowd had left. The kitchen was closed and the ovens were cold, and all that was left to do was fill drink orders. The fireplace crackled, helping all the lanterns in the rafters cast a warm, gilded light over everything. A piper and drummer played on the stage—something pastoral that niggled at the back of Taeva's memory even as it faded to the background beneath all the customers talking. Elawin stood behind the bar, talking to Grams, who was resting in one of the chairs on the customer side. They saw Taeva and her friends walk in and waved, eager expressions on their faces.

The magic of the evening was broken, and it twisted in Taeva's chest. Once again, she plastered her smile into place, ready to go through her usual motions, and started towards the bar. "You two find a seat. I'll be over in a bit."

Her family's faces dropped as soon as they saw her part from her friends. Their waves turned into furious shooing swats, and Taeva stopped in her tracks. She'd expected to come home and help work.

"We can handle it. Go on!" Grams shouted.

Taeva hesitated for another beat, her face frozen in its mask while her brain struggled to understand that she was being dismissed. Then her heart gave a pleasant lurch, and she spun around and rushed to her friends' table before her family could change their minds. Leena and Kellan found an empty place in the corner at the rear of the tavern, and they collapsed into the chairs in a heap of gowns and coattails. Kellan tucked his lute carefully into the corner.

"Now that we have a little privacy," Leena said as Taeva sat down. "Silversage."

"Do you think he knows we heard him?" Taeva asked.

"Yes, but I don't think he cares," was the wizard's reply. "He was talking loud enough for half of his guests to hear."

That made Taeva sit back in her chair. It was so obvious she felt silly for ever worrying at all.

"Do you think he did it?" Kellan asked.

"He couldn't have. Maybe he hired someone, but it wasn't him directly," Leena said.

Kellan's brow creased. "What do you mean he couldn't have?"

"Lord Amberwood coated his blades with poison," Taeva answered. "And the Watch said Amberwood landed a blow on the killer while trying to defend himself. There was a blood trail. They think the actual murderer is already dead."

Kellan crossed his arms, brows lifting into his messy hair. "You know a lot about the case."

He sounded impressed, and Taeva's cheeks warmed. She tried to brush it off, like she hadn't been collecting information about the case like a morbid magpie. "You hear a lot working in a tavern."

"Not on stage," he said. "I feel like we miss everything up there, even though we're in the middle of it all."

Taeva felt her expression curdle into something awkward. "You see the terrible drunk dancers, though," she said, hoping to steer the subject away from the stage.

Kellan's hand slapped down on the table. "Did you two see Lord and Lady Greenshield?"

"Who?" Leena asked.

Kellan launched into a story about the elderly couple and their drunken escapades at the ball. It sounded like the pair were drunk when they arrived and only got further into their cups the longer they stayed. Kellan told the story like he was performing it, and Leena laughed until she was in stitches, but Taeva found herself distracted through most of it. The duo on stage had started playing a tune she knew. It was a jig, and not even a particularly complex one, but it was well known. It was the first thing she'd ever played in a performance setting. And it had been on that very stage. The flute was playing the fiddle part, and Taeva swayed unconsciously with the beat, a sharp twist of longing deep in her chest.

Kellan finished his story, looking to her for comment. "I can't believe they did that," she said. It sounded like a half-hearted response, even to her ears, and his smile fell a little.

"I, ah, I forgot something," Leena said. She shoved her chair back and stalked across the tavern, leaving Taeva and Kellan in a bubble of awkward silence.

"You look lovely tonight," Kellan finally said. A blush colored the apples of his cheeks, faint but still visible in the firelight.

Taeva was certain her blush glowed brighter than the flutist bard's magic. "Thank you," she answered lamely again, eyes falling to her hands on the table.

"I love that dress," he continued, pausing to clear his throat. "It suits you. Really well."

She couldn't bring herself to look back up at him. Her cheeks were on fire, and a goofy grin tugged at her lips. "I bought it yesterday specifically for the ball."

"It's perfect."

She looked up at him then, her heart hammering against her ribs. "You think so?" she whispered.

"Of course." His eyes studied hers for a moment. "Was something bothering you? About my story? I didn't want to offend you."

"No, not at all! It was the music." Flustered, the words came out of her mouth before she could stop them. As soon as she realized what she said, the blush drained out of her, and she wished the floor would open up and swallow her. Regrettably, it did not oblige.

"Were they bad? I haven't been paying attention." Kellan looked to the stage, his focus intent.

"No, nothing like that. They're pretty good. It's just—"

She cut herself off, biting her tongue to keep it from wagging. Why did she want to tell Kellan her every little sorrow? Any interest he might have in her would dry up as soon as he learned what a terrible bard she'd made.

"I don't like that jig they were playing." She sounded pretentious and had to fight to keep from cringing, but it was better than telling him the truth.

He nodded, opening his mouth to say something, but Leena interrupted him by banging three goblets onto the table.

"The autumn mead!" she exclaimed, winking at Taeva.

Taeva playfully rolled her eyes and launched into a brief explanation on how the drink was made. She didn't know the finer details, but the details were boring anyway. From there, Leena tried, and failed, to teach them about potion making. By the time she finally gave up, they were all laughing, goblets empty, a pleasant buzz humming through their veins.

And Taeva didn't look back to the stage. She did, however, steal more glances at Kellan, emboldened by the mead. And he didn't look away. He merely smiled.

Chapter Ten

aeva's head ached a little the next morning, but she didn't regret a thing. At least, not until Grams came down the stairs early, grinning like a cat who'd cornered a mouse. She caught Taeva in the middle of stoking the fire.

"That young man last night sure was handsome," she said.

Taeva jumped and almost dropped the fire poker. She took a steadying breath. "He is," she agreed. It would be impossible to lie about that.

"When's he coming to take you on a date?"

Taeva sighed. "He's not, Grams. He doesn't know anything about me."

"So? That's what dating is for!"

"Yes, but..." She stood, smoothing out her rust-colored skirt. "He's a musician. A really good one. If he knew what I did..." She couldn't bring herself to continue, even though Grams already knew about the incident. She was the only one Taeva had told, though she hadn't given her all the details of how terribly she'd failed. She only knew it hadn't gone how Taeva had wanted. Still, she was the only one Taeva knew who wouldn't judge her for taking a shot at a different life, even if it had gone badly.

"Oh, sugar." Grams hugged her, rubbing her back. "If he finds out about that and it changes the way he looks at you, he's not worth even a drop of cheap ale. *And* I'll whop him with my spoon."

Taeva choked out a laugh. "He should be scared."

"Damn right. Now, perk up. We don't worry over boys."

"Not us. Never," Taeva said, leaning into Grams' embrace for moment. Then, with a deep inhale, she pulled herself back and up and squared her shoulders. Grams gave her an approving nod and one last pat, and they got to work.

They dove into their morning tasks, and with Grams's help, the front door swung open early. The postman came and went with a couple of fresh scones, and customers filed in in a steady stream. Nearly all of their tables and the bar were full during the height of the lunch rush. Taeva worried she'd have to start a waiting list—something that always complicated the day—and was looking toward the door when a pair of women walked in. They were both dressed in livery, but the one who caught Taeva's eye wore the golden yellow and white of the Amberwood family. It glowed in the soft lighting of The Honey Goblet and contrasted beautifully against her dark skin.

Elawin took their orders and directed them to sit at the last open table. Taeva caught a brief snatch of their conversation as they headed to their seats. They were talking about the murder.

Taeva barely kept herself from following them to their seats and grilling the Amberwood stewardess until she'd gleaned every possible detail from the woman. The entire city was still talking about the case, bringing all kinds of gossip into the tavern, but Taeva had never seen this woman. Nor had she had a chance to speak to someone who worked for the late lord.

But being so very interested in the death of a stranger was odd. They wouldn't care to understand that Taeva needed distractions to keep from wallowing in her own self-pity. They'd tell everyone about the ghoulish girl working at The Honey Goblet. It wasn't the kind of attention her family's business needed; it was one thing to ask the Watch about their work and something else entirely to stick her nose into every bit of gossip people brought through the door. The people at the table beside the women gathered their things and headed toward the door. Taeva swooped down on the empty table like a hawk, cleaning up the discarded plates and mugs. And listening.

"I've worked there for so long. I know his entire family. I still can't believe it happened," the woman in the livery said.

"And they still don't know who did it." The other woman shook her head. "You'd think they'd have figured something out by now."

Taeva stacked plates as carefully as she could, hoping not to make too much noise and draw attention to herself.

The liveried woman scoffed. "They should have. I told them exactly who it was. It was Silversage."

Taeva froze, and the woman's friend gasped, her hand lifting to cover her mouth.

"What do you mean?" she asked.

"He was visiting the night before it happened. Unannounced. All fired up about Amberwood wanting to replace the Watch with his own men. Said he would be taking control of the city from the king and that it would be treason dressed up in pretty words and legal documents. I heard it all—I was serving their drinks."

Taeva started wiping down the table, still moving as slowly as she dared. If anyone paused for a moment to pay attention to how long it was taking her, it would be obvious that she was eavesdropping. In her experience, though, people rarely paid attention to what was happening around them. At least that's what a rogue in one of her favorite books had said. She hoped it was true.

"He couldn't have been angry enough to kill Amberwood and attack all those guards, though," the friend said.

"Spitting fire, he was. Make no mistake, though. People like him don't do their own dirty work. They hire someone else to do it for them. Probably hired someone to hire someone to hire someone. Confuse the trail. He'll get away with it, like the nobles always do."

Taeva scooped up the dishes and started for the kitchen, unable to drag her cleaning and eavesdropping out any further. It was just like Leena had said the night before. What if it was Silversage and no one was able to prove it? How many more people would become targets as he climbed his way into more power? She put the dishes in the bin to be washed, chewing on her lower lip.

And what could I even do about it anyway?

TAEVA SPENT THE REST OF THE LUNCH RUSH AND THE afternoon lull thinking about what she'd heard, both from the Amberwood stewardess and from Silversage himself. She considered going to the Watch to report it, but realized she didn't have any real evidence. It was all just gossip. Circumstantial. And if the stewardess had already reported her beliefs—and been ignored—what difference would Taeva repeating her make?

"Don't look now, but we have a visitor," Grams said, a wicked smirk deepening the lines of her face.

"We have visitors all day," Taeva said with a laugh. She turned to the door, then stumbled, catching herself on the bar.

Kellan walked through the door, eyes on her and her alone, smiling. He was dressed casually in dark grey breeches and a cream-colored tunic that laced at the throat. A black coat, worn open, and tall boots completed the outfit, making him look like an adventurer or a mercenary. It was weird not seeing him in formal clothes or motley. Taeva struggled to keep her eyes from drifting to the bit of skin revealed behind the loose laces of the tunic.

Goddesses, it's not fair that he looks so good without trying.

Grams elbowed Taeva, and she nearly jumped out of her skin.

"Kellan," she stammered. "Um, nice to see you! What can I get for you?"

"I wasn't here to order anything, actually." He cast a nervous glance at Grams. "I was wondering if you'd like to go see the other members of my band perform. They've worked up something really special. And I've already asked them not to play the jig you don't like."

Taeva's heart sat in her throat again, and she wasn't certain she was breathing. Grams' early comment about him taking her on a date sprang to mind, and before she could stop herself, she said, "Like a date?"

Kellan passed a hand through his hair and looked between her and Grams. "Uh, yes. I suppose it is, yes."

"She'd love to!" Grams said before Taeva could form words. She pulled at the ties on Taeva's apron. "Get you gone, young lady." She dragged Taeva down so she could pull it over her head.

"Grams," Taeva hissed.

"You'll thank me later. And don't believe all the garbage about modesty—you can absolutely kiss on the first date. How do you think I caught your grandfather?" she whispered.

"Grams!" Taeva exclaimed, bolting back upright, face aflame.

Grams tittered at her and waved them away, sauntering back to the kitchen. "She doesn't have a curfew!" she called over her shoulder.

Taeva looked at Kellan, certain he was already regretting asking her to go anywhere. "I am so sorry," she whispered, hoping Grams wouldn't hear her.

Kellan smiled, so warm she could have melted. "Don't be. She seems great! Nothing like a feisty grandma to keep you on your toes."

Taeva chuckled, some of the tension easing from her shoulders. "That's one word for it."

He gestured toward the door. "Shall we?"

Chapter Eleven

*E*arly afternoon light spilled through the streets, lining everything in a crisp golden glow. The breeze that swept down the street and ruffled Taeva's and Kellan's hair was cool enough to make her grateful she'd grabbed her coat on the way out the door.

Kellan walked beside her, his hands in his pockets. He looked confident and collected, like he did on stage—as though he knew how the afternoon would go as surely as he knew the phrasing in a piece of music. She didn't feel even half as self-assured. A mad fluttering filled her stomach any time she looked in his direction. It eased a little when she looked away. Quietly, she took a deep breath and counted to five before she exhaled, willing her shoulders to relax downward. It was an old trick Madam Tifera had taught her. It worked better now than any time she'd used it in her training, though the tension buzzing through her refused to leave entirely.

"So, your whole family works in the tavern?" Kellan asked, cutting through their awkward silence.

"We do," she said, fidgeting with a button on her bodice. "Father makes the mead and manages everything while Mother, Grams, and I cook and handle the customers."

"I expected your Grams to be in charge of the whole operation."

"She used to be. She handed the books over to Father when I was still little, though. She said she would *not* be bothered with all the numbers and figures ever again."

Kellan chuckled. "Don't blame her there. I can barely keep my own schedule straight. I'd hate to be put in charge of running an entire tavern."

Taeva's smile slipped. *I would hate it, too,* she thought. But all she said in reply was, "It is a lot of work. And a lot of numbers."

"Have you always worked there?" Kellan continued, oblivious that The Honey Goblet was the rain cloud dampening the mood.

Taeva had gotten too good at acting.

"For the most part," she answered, keeping her tone as neutral as she could. She sent up a silent prayer to all the goddesses that he would change the subject. She didn't want to make things awkward by doing it herself.

"I've always loved playing at taverns. It's so much more fun than playing at balls and concerts."

"Really?" Prayer answered. Taeva latched onto the change of subject like it would keep her from drowning.

Kellan nodded. "People are wonderful at the fancier events, don't get me wrong, and there's something to be said for playing a grand, sweeping piece of music with a full orchestra. One that makes an audience cry or leaves them speechless. But in taverns and in the Square it's just *fun*. There's less pressure. I can play anything with a good rhythm, and people will enjoy it. And the dancing. I love the dancing. It reminds me of home."

She lifted her brows, and laughter colored her words. "Your family dances a lot?"

His gaze grew distant, and a sweet kind of sadness tipped

up his lips. "They do. And lots of them play instruments, too. Every family get together is a party."

Taeva tried to imagine a life where family came together without the weight of business hanging over everything and found herself endlessly jealous. She loved her family, she really did. She also couldn't remember a time when they'd all sat down together and hadn't discussed mead, the tavern, or coin in some capacity. It was her family's life. She'd never signed up for it to be hers, too.

She wasn't able to hide the shift in her mood this time. Kellan looked over at her, concern pulling his brows together. She thought he was about to ask what was wrong and she'd have to formulate another excuse, but he looked over her shoulder, his face brightening.

"Want a snack?" he asked.

Before she could answer, he'd grabbed her hand and pulled her toward a pastry shop on the corner. Her skin tingled, and her thoughts garbled together until she couldn't even remember what she'd been so morose about to begin with.

The sign over the door was carved into the shape of a croissant with glossy paint drizzled over it to look like chocolate. When Kellan pushed the door open, the scent of sugar and baking dough enveloped them like a warm embrace. He let go of her to hold the door open for her. Her hand immediately felt cold again, and she tried to ignore the small twinge of disappointment that twisted through her.

A male gnome popped up unto a step stool behind the counter, wiping his hands on his pastel pink apron. Even his violet hair was dusted in flour. "Kellan! It's been two whole days—I was starting to worry."

Kellan smiled bashfully at Taeva. "I might come in here regularly."

"'Bout every single day!" The baker corrected, hands on his hips. "Kid might turn into a pastry if he's not careful. What can I get for you two?"

Taeva looked at the glass display case in front of them. It wrapped around to the right side of the shop, and even more desserts were displayed in a taller case behind the counter.

"I've never seen so much dessert in one place," she said.

The baker beamed. "I have the largest, most experienced group of pastry chefs in the city. Anything you could want, we can bake."

"He's not exaggerating," Kellan said. "But those are my favorite." He pointed to a group of miniature cakes with colorful wrappers and bright pink frosting. They were even topped with sprinkles. "He calls them cupcakes."

"As they are, in fact, baked inside cups," the gnome said, one finger lifted as he clarified.

"I'll try one," Taeva said.

The head baker jumped down and moved to retrieve one for her. "I'll venture a guess that's what you want too, Kellan?"

"Absolutely," Kellan answered.

Taeva gave a very Grams-like snort before she could stop herself.

"What?" Kellan asked with a half-smile and a quirked brow.

"You're dressed like a rogue and asking for the pink sprinkled thing. It's cute."

She froze, eyes going wide and her blush returning with a vengeance.

Kellan's smile didn't falter, but a light blush crept to his cheeks as well. He glanced away quickly, fingers fidgeting with one of the buttons on his coat. "I'm glad you think so."

The way Taeva's stomach flipped, she wasn't sure if she would be able to eat the cupcake at all. The baker handed her the treat over the counter, and she forced herself to take a bite, hoping she looked more collected than she felt.

The icing was strawberry, and pieces of the actual fruit studded the cake itself. The tartness of the fruit tempered the sugariness of the icing, which was whipped to a light, perfect texture.

"Mmm," Taeva hummed, savoring the bite. "I understand why these are your favorite."

Kellan accepted his cake and passed a few coins over the counter before turning back to her. "Wonderful, right?" His eyes landed—and fixated—on her mouth. "You have icing... Here, I'll get it."

He cupped the side of her cheek, brushing icing from the corner of her mouth with the pad of his thumb. Taeva's heartbeat jumped from an easy andante to a surging prestissimo. Then he put his thumb to his mouth, licking it clean. He froze, like his own actions had surprised him. Taeva wondered if she could blush hot enough to burst into flame.

Kellan cleared his throat and hurried to hold the door open for her. "The square where they're performing is right around the corner."

She rushed through the door, still blushing, but smiling so hard her cheeks ached.

THE SQUARE WHERE KELLAN'S DRUMMER AND FLUTIST BARD were performing was a small one. Only about twice the size of The Honey Goblet, it was more of an area for people to relax than a bustling hub for commerce like the Grand Square. A fountain stood in the center, depicting Losharva, goddess of magic, holding her vase aloft, water springing from it to symbolize the wisdom and power she poured into the world. Wrought iron chairs and tables clustered beneath the boughs of grand oaks on the edges of the square. The musicians were set up in front of the fountain, already playing. Taeva took a deep breath as she followed Kellan through the crowd. She could do this. There was no need to be nervous.

How many times did she need to tell herself that before it became true?

Kellan found them a table to sit at while they finished their cakes. "Madam," he said, pulling her chair out for her.

The musicians started playing a lively gigue, a piece Taeva was only passingly familiar with, and people crowded forward to dance. Before the first phrase was even played, laughter filled the air along with the music.

Then, in the fading afternoon light, the bard worked her magic. Swirling ribbons of multi-colored light twirled away from her and soared through the crowd. They danced with the revelers, twining themselves through limbs, circling around couples, and spiraling through the few empty spaces. The magic even moved with some of the lone dancers, giving them a glittering, serpentine partner.

"Wow," Taeva whispered. She watched the lights spinning through the crowd, mystified. "I wish I could do something like that."

"You could!" Kellan said without hesitation. "All it takes is practice and time. I'm sure Miralea would be glad to teach you. She's a great teacher, with flute and magic both."

All of Taeva's joints locked. "Oh, no. I can't," she said, struggling to keep calm.

Kellan popped the rest of his cake into his mouth and wiped his hands on his pants. "Well, I'll be glad to ask her about it if you ever change your mind."

He brushed it off, just a passing thought. The tiny coil of tension in Taeva's gut loosened. The fact that he didn't push, that he backed off immediately to let her decide for herself if she wanted to pursue something or not... She couldn't remember a time anyone had done that for her. She was infinitely grateful.

She looked back toward the dancers and the glowing magic that tangled around them. Heart already pounding, she seized every bit of courage she had and blurted out, "Would you like to dance?" She hoped he wouldn't shoot her down. It would make things so awkward. Or maybe it would be better if he did—she hadn't danced in so long she wasn't sure she remembered how.

His broad smile was all the answer she needed. "I'd love to," he said.

He held out his hand, and Taeva took it, letting him lead her into the swirl of light and people. The music shifted into a fast-paced reel, and they were swept into the spiral of people skipping through the ribbons of magic. Kellan kept one of her hands in his, placing the other at her waist, as he tried and failed to lead them in the dance.

He was a brilliant lutist, but a dancer he was not. He missed steps, fell out of time, and nearly ran into several of the other dancers. If Taeva didn't know better, she would have thought he was drunk. By the third time he stumbled over his own feet, they were close to collapsing in laughter. A purple ribbon figure-eighted itself between them then shot up into the air in a tight spiral.

"I can try leading, if you want," Taeva said, gasping for air as she laughed.

"Lead on," he answered, chuckling at himself good-naturedly.

They did better with her leading, but not by much. The dance had built in speed and intensity, and they stumbled through it, laughing at each other and clinging together for balance every time Kellan misstepped. The reel ended in a dramatic crescendo, and the ribbons whirled together over the crowd's heads, then burst into thousands of twinkling lights that drifted down over them like glittering, rainbow-colored snow.

A collective gasp swept through the crowd before they broke into enthusiastic applause. Taeva held out a hand, catching tiny pieces of the glowing magic. They tingled against her skin as they slowly faded.

The next piece started, slow and romantic, the flute playing long and lingering notes. Glowing orbs appeared overhead, bathing everything in red and gold light. Taeva and Kellan stood in the middle of the crowd while even more couples gathered around them. They all twirled slowly and held each other close. It highlighted how close together she and Kellan stood, his arm still looped around her waist.

His gaze fell to her lips again. She stopped breathing, her pulse zinging like lightning through every vein.

Another couple accidentally brushed against them, and while they didn't notice, it broke the spell Taeva and Kellan were under. He blinked like he was trying to wake himself. "I should probably get you home. It's long past dark," he whispered.

"Alright," Taeva answered. Her disappointment stung again, but she tried to keep it from showing. Him not kissing her certainly didn't ruin the evening. Very few things could have.

Kellan pulled away, the space between them suddenly vast and impassable, but he didn't drop her hand. Instead, he twined their fingers together and led her out of the square. He kept their hands interlaced the entire way back to The Honey Goblet, and Taeva grinned like a fool. She couldn't remember the last time she felt so light or so warm.

Chapter
Twelve

*T*he Honey Goblet was empty by the time they stopped at the front doors. Barely any light shined out of the front windows, the candles extinguished, and Taeva's family was likely already upstairs for the evening. She stood right outside the threshold, awkwardly twisting her hands, unwilling to leave but also unsure what to say.

Kellan cleared his throat. "I had a great time," he said, his voice soft. He tucked his hands into his pockets and rocked on the balls of his feet.

Taeva's cheeks warmed. "So did I."

"I'll see you again soon?" The hope in his voice tugged at Taeva's heart in the most delicious way.

"I'd like that."

He looked down sheepishly. Seeing him so self-conscious should have given her a bit of a confidence boost, but it did just the opposite. Her pulse stacattoed when he opened his mouth to say something else, then closed it with a snap. Then it rushed when he reached out and gently tucked a lock of her hair behind her ear.

"Have a good night," he said.

He turned and started to walk away while Taeva struggled to find her voice. "You too!" she blurted. He smiled over his shoulder, and she could have turned into a puddle on the spot.

It was a very gentlemanly goodbye, but somehow still raffish despite their nerves. And he wanted to see her again. Soon! The thought warmed her as she locked the doors behind her.

Taeva crept up the stairs, skipping the third and seventh steps to avoid the loud squeaks they always made. The stairs ended at a hallway that extended in both directions. She ignored the conversation drifting from the living room on the left and turned to go the other way. She tip-toed across the worn hardwood floors, then ducked into the second door on the right. Her room.

She bristled with a crackling energy, her emotions still soaring after such a lovely evening, and she channeled it into near reckless courage. The music and magic the flutist made inspired her, and she needed to act on it. She was going to play the violin. Not where anyone would hear her, and she wasn't brave enough to try anything magical, but she was going to play.

She grabbed the case propped up in the corner and retreated back downstairs. Her palms were already sweaty as she closed the door to the stairs.

She laid the case on the bar and, taking a deep breath, undid the latches. A dark green cloth rested over the instrument, and she drew it aside. There it was. The instrument that had brought her so much joy and then so much pain.

It looks … sad, she thought as she stared down at it.

The last time she'd touched her violin, right after the incident, she'd loosened the strings and pulled off the bridge, not wanting anything to warp while it was stored away, even if she'd had no intention to ever play it again. She'd even considered selling it, but hadn't been able to bring herself to do it in the end. Her parents bought the violin for her from the Overhollows' shop on her twelfth birthday. Her first full-sized instrument. It was old, but well cared for, and the wood sang, deep and resonant. She'd loved it from the very first time she'd drawn the bow across the strings. She hated that it had spent four months tucked away like it didn't matter.

Her hand trembled as she reached for the bow tucked into the lid of the case. Her fingers closed around it, the weight so familiar it was like an extension of her own arm. She started turning the knob on the bow to tighten the hair and gasped.

She wasn't in the tavern anymore, but outside of a goblin cave. There was a screech—a bow pulled over the strings with an overly-tense hand. A flash of sickly yellow-green light. Screams of panic.

She loosened the bow in a rush, then tucked it away with shaking, unsteady hands. She barely remembered to replace the silk cloth before slamming the lid to the case shut again.

"I can't do it," she whispered to herself as she fought to catch her breath. She slumped onto a stool. "I can't."

She stayed there until the pounding in her chest eased, then flipped the latches closed. Her hands started shaking again just handling the case, panic rising like water around her, so she stashed it under the bar.

It'll be fine there, she told herself as she mounted the stairs. *Just fine.*

HER FAILURE TASTED LIKE ASH ON HER TONGUE THE NEXT morning as she went through her banal routine. She determined as she stoked the fire that she would try to play again, hoping to stoke courage into herself as the flames licked back to life. Her hands trembled at the mere thought, and she closed them into fists. She wasn't sure when, but she would try again.

Leena came through the front door right as Taeva's family came down the stairs. She was back in her Academy robes, and her backpack looked ready to burst at every seam. She leaned forward as she walked, trying to balance out the weight of it.

"Leena!" Tirson called, delighted. "Come to learn more about mead making? We're going to have to put you on the payroll."

"Not today, I'm afraid." She dropped her bag onto one of the back tables with a thud. "I need to study. They're about ready to give up on the Head Wizards helping with the hunt for the murderer, so classes will be starting again soon."

"Ah, maybe later, then." Tirson waved and disappeared into the kitchen, on his way into the cellar already.

"Can you get the kitchen fires going before you start?" Grams asked. "It's such a help."

"Sure!" Leena trailed Grams into the kitchen.

Taeva had just sat down behind the bar when Leena burst back into the main room.

"You went on a date with Kellan?" she squealed. "Were you not going to tell me?"

"Of course I was," Taeva said, sighing. "Grams beat me to it."

Leena pulled out a stool across from her and perched on the edge, leaning forward on the bar. "Tell me everything."

So Taeva did. They both laughed as she recounted Kellan's terrible dancing, and her cheeks ached from smiling by the time she was finished.

Leena draped herself onto the bar even more dramatically, her hands dangling off the other side. "I can't believe he didn't kiss you. It would have been perfect."

"Maybe. But it was still pretty close to perfect without it."

"Not a single rakish bone in his body," Leena lamented.

"That's not a bad thing!"

"Depends on who you're asking, I suppose," Leena said, waggling her brows. "Are you going to go out with him again?"

"I hope so. He said he had a busy few days, but that I'd see him again soon."

"If he doesn't, I'm going to beat him with his own lute."

Taeva rolled her eyes. "Be serious."

"You're right. I'll light him on fire," Leena said, laughing. "You know, he used to come into the shop with his cousins all the time, even before he started playing the lute." Her eyes drifted to the ceiling. "One of them played the lyre. I can't remember the other. But they were all so loud. That I do remember. Played loud, spoke loud, everything loud. It was such a good break in the monotonous quiet in the shop."

Taeva looked at her friend, lifting a brow. "You might be the only wizard in the world that prefers chaos to peace and quiet."

Leena shrugged. "Magic itself is the chaos of creation. I'm merely submitting to its nature. Embracing it." She wiggled her fingers, and sparks danced across them.

Their first customers for the day walked in—a trio of elf women in fine clothing, their hair and skin all so pale they were almost translucent. Taeva shooed Leena away from the bar.

"Go study, mighty wizard. It's time for work."

Leena retreated to her table with a wave. Taeva went to work with grim resolve, but she felt lighter. Her failure with her violin the night before didn't weigh so heavy on her mind thanks to her friend's distraction. Even when she caught glimpses of it behind the bar, she was able to easily push it from her mind. She wondered if, somehow, without even trying, she was healing. Like every tiny step she took closer to music made all the others easier.

Taeva swooped past Leena's table on her way back from delivering food to Bartley Smeltiron and his apprentices. She placed a goblet on the table in one of the few empty spaces left between all the books and parchment.

"What's this?" Leena asked.

"Father's new experiment. Nonalcoholic cider. He's hoping it'll be a new seasonal drink for people who don't want a drink-drink when they have to go back to work."

Leena took a sip, and her face crumpled like she'd sucked on a lemon. "That's... I can't lie to you, that's terrible. Your father might need to go back to the drawing board. It doesn't taste like alcohol, but it's *bitter*. Ugh." She passed the glass back to Taeva.

"I don't think he's ever had a new drink flop that hard," she said, staring down at the cider. She dreaded the thought of bringing him the news. He'd clearly been so confident in it that he hadn't felt the need to taste it for himself.

"It happens to everyone. Even the Head Wizards when they're inventing new spells," Leena said, nonchalant, before turning back to her books.

"I'll bring you something else," Taeva muttered and turned away, still studying the glass of failed drink.

Leena stayed through the lunchtime rush, her stacks of books and papers multiplying as time went on, as if by magic. When the tavern started to quiet down around midafternoon, Taeva noticed Leena growing more and more distracted until, finally, with a dramatic sigh, her friend stared packing her books.

"Not loud enough anymore?" Taeva asked as Leena walked back up to the bar, backpack bowing her spine again.

"No, sadly." She swung around to the back of the bar and put her empty goblet in the bin with the others that needed to be washed. "Don't forget to tell your father about that cider."

Taeva grimaced. She'd been putting that off, and clearly, Leena had noticed. "I will. It's going to ruin his whole day."

"He'll fix it easily enough, I'm sure," Leena said, then her eyes snagged on something behind the counter. "Is that your violin?"

Taeva gave a sharp inhale, apprehension pulling her shoulders high and tense. She held her breath for a second, waiting for the roil of panic, but it never came. She exhaled with a sigh. "It is," she answered, surprised at how easy it was to say.

"Have you been playing again?"

"I tried, but ... not yet," she answered. Discussing it wasn't pleasant. There was still an ache in her chest, but she *was* talking about it. It felt like another win.

Tension bracketed Leena's mouth, like she didn't want to say what came next. "Want me to take it to the shop? Mother can give it a once-over—a quick tune-up."

Taeva hesitated. She'd never liked being without it. It shouldn't matter now since she hadn't played in so long, but somehow it still did.

Just shows I was never ready to give it up at all, she thought.

But then again, if last night was any indicator, she wasn't ready to pick it up again either. Maybe, though, if she spent a little coin on it and got it sounding its best, she'd be more likely to make another attempt.

"Yes," she answered before she could talk herself out of it. She squeezed her eyes shut. She had to force her next words out, but once she got started, they flooded forth beyond her control. "I want to play again. And I want it to be in good condition when I do."

Leena's expression softened. "Absolutely. I'll take it to her and tell her to make it top priority."

Between the lull in customers and Leena's departure, Taeva had no more excuses. She had to go down to the cellar and tell her father the cider was a flop. *Had* to. Still, she found herself at the top of the stairs, Leena's discarded glass in one hand, unable to put the next foot forward.

Elawin was kneading bread at a nearby counter. She didn't stop her work but asked, "Something wrong, dear?"

Taeva hid her trepidation behind a more pleasant expression, hoping her mother hadn't noticed the grimace that flashed across her face. "No, I thought I was forgetting something." She took off at a trot down the stairs, all but hurling herself into the colder air below before Elawin could ask her any more questions.

There would be a lecture coming, she knew it. The worst one yet, since her father would already be upset over the cider. *Lyria, give me the grace to weather it,* she thought as she took her first step into the cellar.

"Father?"

Tirson looked up from where he stood at one of the tables, bent over one of his many ledgers. "Ah! The cider," he said, beaming. "How did our wizarding friend like it?"

Taeva set the nearly-full drink onto the table and watched as it sloshed a little in the glass. She couldn't meet his gaze. "She said it was bitter. She didn't like it."

"What?" Tirson picked up the drink and inhaled deeply. "It has a bit of a bitter smell, but that doesn't necessarily mean..." Taeva looked up as he took a sip. His face crumpled, just like Leena's had, and he sputtered. "Goddesses, it is rank. Where in the world did I go wrong? The apples were the perfect ripeness..." He trailed off, turning to the wall where the rest of the records were kept.

Taeva took half a step back, hope blossoming in her chest. If he plunged himself straight into trying to fix it, she might get away without any lambasting over her lack of involvement in the brewing. It seemed too good to be true, but he kept muttering to himself as she turned. She was almost to stairs when her hope shattered.

"Say, you don't think there's anything magical that could fix this, do you, honey?" She glanced over her shoulder to find him watching her over the top of his glasses, several ledgers in his arms already. "Something that would fix the entire batch? Save us some time and money?"

"I'll ask Leena the next time I see her."

Tirson tilted his head. "I meant with a little tune."

"Oh." Taeva was so shocked she struggled to form even that pitiful response.

Her father cleared his throat and continued. "Yes, I think you could. I've seen you do more complicated things than that. What do you say, honey?"

"I..." She remembered the tingle of magic in her fingertips and squeezed her hands into tight fists. Playing a little bit of music was one thing; attempting a spell was something else entirely. It was too much too soon—overwhelming to the point that it threatened to choke her. If she tried a spell, there was every possibility that she could burn her family's home to the ground. Or turn the entire thing into a giant pastry. She wasn't sure which would be worse. "I don't do that kind of thing anymore," she blurted out.

She turned on her heel and stormed up the stairs before Tirson could respond, her heart hammering against her ribs. She sped through the kitchen, taking deep, gasping breaths. With one last giant pull of air, she had her performing face back in place before she burst out behind the bar.

It was over. It was done. She could hardly believe Tirson had paid her a compliment about something other than mead and the tavern, but she was past it. No more thoughts of magic. She was ready to move on.

She smiled, maybe a little too brightly, at the pair of gnomes who'd hopped onto stools at the counter. "What can I get for you two?"

Chapter Thirteen

A few days later, the post-runner pushed through the front doors of The Honey Goblet the moment Taeva unlocked them. He had documents for Tirson and, to her complete surprise, two letters for Taeva. She tipped the runner with one of Grams' biscuits, then tucked her father's documents under one arm as she made her way back to the bar.

She wasted no time opening her letters—she'd already started a small collection of notes from Kellan; hopefully one of these was another. She grinned, thinking about the first two.

TAEVA,

I had a great time. I know I already said that, but I really did. I want to see you again. Soon. I hope you still feel the same way.
    Kellan

TAEVA,

I was asked to play that reel we danced to at a gig last night. I think I figured out where my feet went wrong in the dance. I can't wait to try it again.
    Kellan

. . .

She tore open the first envelope. It was from Overhollow Fine Instruments, saying her violin was ready to pick up today. The thought made her stomach flip, but she took a few deep breaths, and it settled again. She'd worked her courage up over the past few days, thinking about her trip to the Grand Square with Leena and going dancing with Kellan. She'd balked in both instances, but only briefly, and she hadn't fled either time. It'd been good to be around music like that again—to enjoy it. And she missed her instrument. She was ready to try again.

She deposited Tirson's post on the table at the back of the kitchen, then opened her next letter. Her stomach flipped again. The writing across the front was quickly becoming as familiar to her as her own. It was another letter from Kellan.

Taeva,

I have a gig near you in a couple of days. I'd love to see you afterward, or on every break I get, if you're not too busy working.

Kellan

Taeva read the letter three times, grinning like a fool. For three days, she'd fretted over if and when he'd ask to see her again. She'd confided the same to Leena the day before.

"He's got two fatal flaws," the wizard had answered, ticking them off on her fingers. "He's booked to death. Double and triple booked sometimes even. We've had patrons of his looking for him at the shop. And he's every bit the whimsical, flakey artist." She rolled her eyes. "I'll still break his lute over his head if he upsets you. Fire is also still on the table."

Warmth suffused Taeva's chest as she replayed the memory. There would be no need to damage instruments after all. She'd drop a reply off to the postmaster on her way to the Overhollow's shop later in the day. Because she was going to pick up her violin. And she *was* going to play it. Tonight.

She hoped.

The day breezed by in a whirl of anxious energy mixed with breathless, hopeful anticipation, both about her violin and seeing Kellan. She left the tavern in the lull between lunch and dinner, her feet carrying her through the streets to the luthier shop with hardly a thought. How many times had she walked this path before, both with her parents and on her own? It had to be in the hundreds.

Autumn had come on in earnest, and the crisp wind that blew down the cobblestoned lanes carried fallen golden leaves in its wake. Taeva pulled her collar up, smiling as she walked under a line of trees. They still held on to most of their leaves, and the riot of yellows, oranges, and reds had always been one of her favorite things about this time of year. It was like the trees had their own magic and were putting on a grand show before they rested at the end of the year. She dropped off her letter to Kellan, then skipped through a pile of leaves, giggling.

She'd always loved sitting under the trees and playing, her violin playing backup for nature's own music. Maybe that wasn't lost to her after all. With everything she'd done in the last couple of weeks, it was starting to feel like it was once again in her grasp.

As long as I can stomp the magic down if it tries to rise...

The thought sobered her as she rounded a bend and Overhollow Fine Instruments came into view. It felt a little like she was marching into battle as she took the last few steps up to the door and let herself inside, a tuning fork above the door ringing out a perfect A note.

The shop hadn't changed since the first time Taeva had set foot in it as a child, and the familiarity of it hit her with enough force to knock the wind from her lungs. The long open room stretched out in front of her, broken by a half-wall near the front that divided a small sitting area from the working area of the shop. Violins, violas, cellos, lutes—every manner of string instrument—hung from the walls in various states of repair, some complete, others in parts as hide glue or varnish dried. Wood shavings covered one of the tables and the floor around it where a cello back was being carved. It smelled like wood and leather, and Taeva took a deep breath, soaking it in even as she picked at the fraying edge of her apron.

"I'll be with you in a moment," a soft, feminine voice called through the door at the rear of the room. Taeva settled into the worn leather sofa at the store front to wait.

She wasn't waiting long. Leena's mother came out of the back room carrying three long, narrow blocks of wood. An elf, Carinthyra Overhollow was as tall and graceful as the spruce trees she used to make her instruments. Her skin was a rich, dark brown, and her nearly-black hair was worn in a sleek braid that she coiled up into a bun. Taeva had long suspected she was old, even by elven standards, because of the faint care lines around her eyes and mouth, but her gaze was still as sharp as her carving tools. No detail was too small for her to pick up on.

"Taeva, dear, how are you?" She put the wood down next to the half-carved cello and moved to stand behind the short dividing wall where Taeva remembered they kept the coin box and the instruments that were ready to be sent home.

"I'm well, thank you. The new cello looks like it's coming

along great," Taeva said, fighting to keep her voice steady. She knew what would be coming next, and even though she told herself she was ready, it didn't make her any less nervous. "The flame on the maple is gorgeous."

It wasn't an exaggeration. The way the light hit the wood looked like the ripple of sunlight on water. When Carinthyra varnished the instrument and the contrast in the grain deepened, it would be stunning.

The luthier smiled, the faint lines in the corners of her eyes deepening. "The wood makes it pretty. I only hope I can make it sound as good as it looks."

"I'm sure you will," Taeva said, meaning every word. She'd never known Leena's mother to do anything less than exemplary work.

"Here is your baby," she said, changing the subject and setting Taeva's case on the counter. She opened the lid and removed the silk cover. "I didn't have to do much, just a new bridge and new strings. The sound post fell when you took it down for storage, but I adjusted that, and it's ready to go."

"It looks great." Taeva swallowed. Maybe she could get out of here without testing it if she steered the conversation just right. She would try playing again, but she didn't want an audience. "How much do I owe you?"

"Nothing at all. Leena asked that I do this as a favor to her friend. She's never asked for that before." Her gaze grew misty, and she paused to push the case a little closer to Taeva. "She spends so much of her spare time studying that she's never had time for much else. Socializing hasn't been on her priorities list. And I understand you're picking the instrument back up after a break. It's been too long since we've gotten to hear you play. You're beautifully skilled. It shouldn't go to waste."

Tears pricked the back of Taeva's eyes. "That's too kind."

"I'm only stating the facts. Now, give it a play to make sure you like the tone, and you can be on your way."

Sweat slicked Taeva's palms, and she cast her eyes around the shop, looking for any excuse to get away. Her gaze fell on the cello again. "I don't want to keep you from your work."

"Nonsense," Carinthyra said. She took out Taeva's bow and tightened the hair. "It's part of my work to make sure everyone leaves satisfied." She studied Taeva for a moment, and her expression softened. "Just some open strings to make sure it's how you like it." She held the bow out to Taeva in invitation.

"Alright," she answered, voice trembling.

She swallowed hard and reached for the bow. Her fingers curled around the frog of their own accord, falling into place like they had thousands of times before. Carinthyra unbuckled the violin from where it was held firmly in place against the cushion of the case and held it out for her next. Taeva forced her left hand to reach for it and took it by the neck. Her fingers hit the strings as she did, and the sound vibrated in her chest so hard she worried she would crumble apart.

In a motion that was more of a flinch than anything voluntary, she flipped the violin and snugged it up beneath her chin. It felt natural. Like it was a part of her body. And it should—she'd spent most of her life just like this. The smooth wood tucked under her chin and rested against her collarbone like it wanted to be there.

A few open notes, she repeated to herself. *Just the strings. I don't even need to put any fingers down.*

She squeezed her eyes shut, and as her heart hammered against her ribs like it was trying to break free, she pulled the bow across the thickest string—the G.

The violin vibrated under her jaw as the deep note carried through the shop. Her hand was too tense on the bow, and she could hear it in the tone of the note, but she'd done it. Her eyes flew open, and she looked to Carinthyra, stunned. The elf nodded, smiling softly, and gestured for Taeva to continue.

She grinned back, her hand on the bow softening as she started drawing it across the D string. This time, with the tension in her hand gone, the note rang clear and true, filling the shop. The sound lifted into the ceiling, and it felt like it was carrying her heart with it. The tuning fork over the door chimed an A, and Taeva moved the bow to that string, ready to copy the note.

"Taeva?"

Her bow skidded across the A string with a screech as she whirled around. Kellan stood in the doorway, still holding the door open. He was dressed like he had been on their date, in a neutral tunic and breeches with his black coat open. His already messy dark hair was even more wild, wind-swept by the autumn breeze. He carried his lute with him, the strap pulling tight across his shoulders. He looked good—he always looked good—but Taeva couldn't say she was happy to see him. Not here. Not right now.

"I didn't know you played! Why didn't you tell me?" He didn't look hurt by the revelation. Instead, he was smiling as he let the door close behind him.

"It never came up," Taeva stammered out. She put the violin and her bow back in their case, then rubbed her sweating hands on the skirt of her dress. Her heart was back to hammering at its cage.

Everything was ruined. He'd find out about what she did, how she'd failed, and he wouldn't want to talk to her anymore. He'd tell Leena, and she would be so angry she'd stop coming to study at the tavern. It was over. All the joy she'd found in the last month drained from her in an instant.

He tilted his head and feigned annoyance, brows creasing though he fought to keep from smirking. "Oh, there were plenty of times you could have mentioned it." He couldn't hide his delight for long, though, and his eyes danced. "We should play together! There are lots of fun duets for lute and violin. I—"

"No. No, sorry, I can't," Taeva said. She took two panicked steps towards the door, then whirled to face Carinthyra. "I'm so sorry." Then she bolted past Kellan and through the door.

The sound of the tuning fork chime was like an arrow straight through her heart as she fled into the street.

Chapter Fourteen

"Taeva? Taeva, wait!" Kellan called.

Distantly, she heard the door chime again as he followed her out of the shop, but she didn't stop. She walked as fast as her legs could carry her, trying not to cause a scene. She didn't want people to think she was running from Kellan. He hadn't done anything wrong. She was just ... fleeing. Maybe from herself. Maybe from music. She didn't want to think about it too hard. She didn't want to be there anymore.

"Taeva, what's wrong?" His voice was closer, but she still plowed ahead.

Wrapping her arms tight across her chest, she blinked back hot tears. *I won't cry, I won't cry, I won't cry.*

She turned a sharp corner and slammed to a halt. A long trade caravan rumbled by, clattering over the cobbled street in a riot of sound. The horses pulling the carts moved at a quick trot, more than one breaking into a canter as they whipped through the street. Taeva huddled at the edge of the street, forced to stand and wait for them to pass. Crests adorned all the wagons—a white rose on a deep green field. They gusted by, stirring her skirts and blowing pieces of her hair out of its bun.

And Kellan, of course, caught up to her. She couldn't help the tear that streaked down her cheek.

"Hey, what's wrong?" Kellan asked. He reached his hand

out and slowly put it on her shoulder. In his other hand, he carried her violin case—that damned thing. "Are you alright?"

She nodded, dashing the tear away with the back of her hand. She pulled herself straight and took a deep breath as she looked up at him. He gazed down at her with so much concern, the corners of his mouth tilted down, his dark eyes searching hers like he'd find some mysterious injury. He would hate her if he knew what had happened the last time she'd played, she just knew it.

She opened her mouth to tell him that yes, she was fine, but all that came out was a strangled, "No."

"Oh, goddesses. Hey, whatever it is, it'll be alright."

She shook her head, blinking back more frustrated tears.

"I know what you need," he said. "Tea. Maybe a croissant. Let me buy you some?"

He ended with a questioning lilt, letting her know she could refuse and he wouldn't force her. But, damnit, she didn't want to refuse, even if she knew she should. She nodded, too worried she would burst into wrenching sobs if she opened her mouth.

"Alright, this way. I know the perfect place."

He put his hand on her back, right beneath her shoulder blades, and steered her to the right. He kept his hand there, leading her with gentle nudges and occasionally rubbing a soothing circle through her coat. She chewed on the inside of her lip. She was so embarrassed, both by being caught in the luthier's and by her melodramatic flight, that she couldn't even enjoy his closeness.

He led her to a cafe only a few streets away from the Grand Square. The sign above the door showed a book, open and laying flat, with a swirl of steam and leaves rising from the pages. It read, "Leaves: Tea and Pages." The door swung open silently, and Kellan held it for her and waited for her to walk in.

"This is too expensive," she croaked out. Anything this close to the Square would cost several days worth of tips.

"Shhh," Kellan said, nodding his head for her to go in. "I've been wanting to bring you here all week anyway. In you go."

She walked through into a clean, bright cafe as she sniffled and dashed more tears off her cheeks. An L-shaped counter took up the left side of the long room, its dark wood top polished to a high shine. White iron tables with glass tops filled the space in front of the bar and to the left of the door. A stage took up the corner on the right, made of the same dark wood as the counter and trimmed in gold. Past the counter, in the very back of the cafe, the walls were filled with book shelves. Soft-looking arm chairs and sofas in robin's egg blue sat between the shelves, ready for readers to get comfortable as they got lost in their books. A few people were already doing just that, steaming cups of tea sitting on nearby side tables.

A tall half-orc man with greyish skin and matching hair smiled at them from behind his small, round spectacles. "Your usual, Kellan?" he asked, reminding Taeva of the gnome at the bakery.

Kellan gave him a lopsided, self-depreciating grin. "Always. Any idea what you'd like?" he asked Taeva.

"What's your usual?" After the cupcakes, she expected it would be something sweet and colorful. She wasn't sure her stomach could handle it at that moment.

"A vanilla black tea with a honey scone."

Taeva cocked her head. It surprised her that he would make such a tame request often enough for it to be his usual. And it sounded like exactly what she needed. "That sounds perfect," she said with a sniff.

"I'll have it for you in a moment," the baristo said.

Taeva let Kellan guide her to the table in the front corner. He pulled her chair out for her again before settling into the seat across from her. His lute case got propped up in the corner behind him, but he laid Taeva's violin case across the side of the table closest to the wall. Taeva eyed it like it was a viper that was ready to strike them at any moment.

"Carinthyra said it was ready to go, so I didn't think you'd want to leave it behind," Kellan said. He was watching her like she was a horse, ready to bolt from her imaginary serpent.

It was a punch in the gut. How could she have left her violin behind? It felt like she'd betrayed her oldest friend, even if there was hardly a safer place it could have been. "Thank you."

Awkward silence fell over them, broken only by the sounds of the baristo preparing their orders. One of the other customers in the back of the cafe stood up and replaced the book they'd been reading, only to pull out another one and settle back down to read more.

Taeva ran her fingers over the glass table top. "Tables like this are expensive. It's hard to spin the glass out this far. Father looked into them for the tavern, but we would have needed about twenty of them to fill the entire room. We couldn't afford it."

She fought not to cringe at herself. *Talking about glass? Really?*

Kellan latched onto the subject, though, clearly relieved that the silence was over. "This place has always been fancy. My mom has worked here since I was little. All kinds of rich folks come in. They hire me every now and then to play." He nodded towards the stage. "I have to play all the slow, soft, boring stuff, but the pay and the tips are always worth it."

"Order ready, Kellan," the baristo said. He placed two matching saucers and tea cups on the counter, then went back to his own book.

Kellan jumped up and grabbed their tea and scones. "Milady," he said, handing Taeva hers. She smiled at the blue and white floral dishes. The handle on the tea cup was so fine it vanished in Kellan's fingers as he lifted it to take a sip. "Ah, exquisite as always."

And it was. The tea was expertly steeped, the vanilla perfectly balanced with the black tea leaves. It was even the ideal sipping temperature. The baristo definitely knew what he was doing. They ate and drank in silence for a while, Taeva picking at the scone even though it was just as delicious as the tea.

"Do you want to talk about what happened?" Kellan finally asked. His voice was so gentle it made Taeva feel even worse for running out on him.

She took a deep, steadying breath and wrapped her hands around her cup. "No, but I will." She forced herself to meet his gaze.

"Why did you run?"

There was hurt in his eyes, and Taeva hated that she'd put it there. She looked down again. She wouldn't be able to tell him while he looked at her that way. "I didn't want you to find out that I played. But you walked in and caught me, so I panicked."

"I didn't mean to upset you," he offered. There was so much sincerity in his tone it brought tears back to Taeva's eyes.

"It's not your fault," she said, fighting to blink them away. "I didn't want you to know. I've been too scared to play because of what happened the last time..." She took a deep breath, squirming in her chair. If she could play a little in front of Carinthyra, she could tell Kellan the whole truth. If he hated her afterwards... Well, she'd deal with that if and when it happened.

"I'm a bard, too." She tried to ignore the way his eyes lit up. "I left the city because my parents were putting more and more pressure on me about taking over the tavern. I've never wanted to do that. I love music, not mead. And definitely not all the numbers and calculations that come with running a business. We had a fight—a bad one—and I left the next day."

"Did you go far?" Kellan asked.

Taeva laughed at herself. "No. One city over to Brineport. I was playing in their city square and living in the inn. It was going fine until a group of adventurers asked me if I was a bard."

"And you are."

"I am..." She trailed off, stealing herself for what came next. "But I'm not a good one. I—I don't know why, but I get so nervous I mess up spells more often than not. But I lied to them, or didn't tell them the entire truth, I guess, and they hired me to help them clear out some goblins."

Kellan leaned back in his chair, eyes wide. "Goblins? That's dangerous."

"I know, but I was so sure I could do it. I'd been making it on my own—no parents, no tavern to fall back on. I figured I was over whatever issues I had." She squeezed her eyes shut. "I wasn't. I turned one of the adventurers into a frog by mistake."

He froze, teacup halfway to his mouth and eyes wide. "Goddesses... A frog? Really?"

She opened her eyes and looked at him, pleading with

every goddess that she could name that he wouldn't hate her. "I don't even know if he ever changed back! By some miracle, no one was hurt badly—other than being a frog. It was close. The battle turned into complete chaos after my spell went bad, but the Reavers are true professionals. They still got their job done. But they fired me—they were so angry. And I came home. This all happened five months ago. I haven't played since. I'm too scared about what might happen. Magic has always been quick to rise to my music, and if it does, I might not be able to control it. If I don't play, I can't have a spell go bad. Today was the first time I've even touched the violin again."

She fell silent, returning to methodically tearing her scone into the tiniest pieces possible. Kellan's hand fell over hers, and she jumped, looking back up at him. There was no anger in his expression. No judgement. He looked like he *understood*.

"I can't tell you how many times I've been so nervous on stage that I ended up messing up my part so badly that it threw off everyone playing with me. And I wasn't facing down goblins." He rubbed his thumb across her knuckles, a thoughtful look crossing his face. "I can't understand all that you're feeling, but I can tell you this. I just heard you play— not much, but I did. And so did Carinthyra. And we aren't frogs."

He smiled that lopsided smile again, and Taeva choked out a laugh. "Give it time." She swiped at another errant tear with her free hand, loathe to move the one Kellan held.

"So I'm guessing, since you had your instrument checked on, that you want to play again," he said, lifting his brows.

Taeva nodded. "I do. I'm scared ... but I miss it."

Kellan gave her hand a squeeze, excitement dancing in his dark gaze. "Then it's settled."

She cocked her head, quirking a quizzical brow at him even as her heart wobbled. "What is?"

"You *will* play again. And I'll be there to help, if you want it."

"What? Like lessons?"

"If you want them. I have a feeling you don't need them, though. All you need is a good accompaniment."

THEY FINISHED THEIR TEA, THEN ORDERED ANOTHER ROUND. Taeva felt lighter than she had in months. The food even tasted better, and she scarfed down her scone so fast it embarrassed her after the fact.

Kellan didn't seem to notice. He was too busy delightedly planning for them to meet up again the next day to play. He wanted to work out every detail of their plans, down to what key signature she wanted to work on first. Taeva was too busy stuffing her face to make any comments, but his enthusiasm warmed her even more than the tea.

She'd taken the first step back toward her instrument on her own, but it was a relief to know that she didn't have to walk the rest of the path by herself.

As more customers started to file in for the evening, they returned their dishes and waved goodbye to the brilliant tea-maker. Then they went back out into the crisp autumn air. Taeva carried her case in one hand, and the other was held firmly in Kellan's, their fingers laced together as he steered them through the busy streets.

"I've always heard that violinists think in sharps. Do you want to start in a key with lots of sharps?"

Taeva laughed. "Not even a little. We can start in C major, I think. Is that easy on the lute?" She had no idea how a lute was even tuned.

Kellan opened his mouth to answer, but a door swung open in front of them with enough force that the bell over the shop door sounded like it would break off its chain. A familiar half-orc man stepped out in the street, nearly running into them. He swerved at the last second, a package tucked tight against his chest. He glared at them, then spun away, stalking off and disappearing in the crowd.

Taeva and Kellan stood for a moment in stunned silence.

"Was that Lord Silversage?" Kellan asked.

"I think so. And he sure left in a hurry. Nothing like almost being run over." Taeva leaned to the side to get a better look at the sign above the door. "An apothecary shop."

"Why would he be leaving in such an angry rush?" Kellan mused, looking through the front windows.

He turned back to face her, and Taeva met his gaze, afraid to even say her suspicion out loud. "Do you think they sell poison antidotes?" she whispered.

Silversage was happy Amberwood had been killed— maybe even happy enough to have risked it himself. Maybe driven enough to leave a trail of wounded, innocent guards behind him. And maybe determined enough to risk poisoned blades after all, especially if the antidote was easily available.

She needed to report this to Leena. There had to be something they could do, and her wizard friend would be sure to know where they should start.

"*C*an I talk to you, or is it a bad time?" Taeva
asked.

Leena heaved a dramatic sigh and closed the thick tome
she was bent over with a weighty thud. She pushed it away
from herself, a wry twist to her lips. "Now's fine. It's getting
too quiet in here anyway."

The dinner rush was over, and Leena was right: it was so
quiet they could even hear the crackling of the fire in the
center hearth. There were only a few tables still occupied,
and they all looked like they were wrapping up. The patrons
were talking softly, like they knew everything was winding
down for the night. Tirson hadn't hired any musicians to
play that evening, so the tavern would probably be closing
early.

"I ran into Kellan when I went to pick up my violin
yesterday," Taeva started.

"Oh, did you?" Leena laced her fingers together and
lifted a brow. "Do go on."

Taeva gave her a pointed look before continuing. "That's
not the part I wanted to talk about. On the way back here,
we saw Lord Silversage. He was coming out of an apothecary shop, and he was acting weird."

Leena dropped her teasing expression, a serious one
taking its place. "Weird like suspicious, or weird like sick?"

"Suspicious. He had whatever he bought tucked up

against him like he didn't want anyone to see it, and he all but ran away."

"Hmm." Leena leaned back and crossed her arms. "I wonder if someone at his house is sick, and he doesn't want anyone to know."

"Or poisoned," Taeva said.

Leena's eyes shot up to meet Taeva's gaze, the implication hanging taut between them.

"Should we tell someone?" Taeva finally asked. "They could at least search his house. He had it all locked up as tight as a vault when he had the ball, but the Watch will be able to go through every room."

"I'll take it to the Head Wizards. If they think it's enough to go on, they can report it. The information will carry more weight coming from them."

Taeva nodded. "That makes sense." The Watch was much more likely to listen to one of the Head Wizards than an apprentice and a barmaid. Somehow, though, spreading the information around made her uneasy. "And none of them would be in on it ... right?"

Leena looked offended. "Goddesses, no! It would violate so many oaths in the Wizard's Code!"

"What would?" a familiar voice asked.

Taeva turned to see Kellan walking up, his lute on his back like always. He was dressed in green and silver motley that brought out the warm highlights in his hair.

"Taeva was telling me about the interesting encounter you two had yesterday with a certain lord," Leena said. She explained her plan for reporting the information.

"Works for me," Kellan said. "I have enough on my plate without adding conspiracies and political murders to the list."

"What are you doing here anyway?" Leena asked.

Kellan looked to Taeva, giving her the choice to explain about the violin or make some other excuse. She could have kissed him right then, just for that.

"He's going to help me get back to playing," Taeva answered.

Leena's face lit up. "That's great! You love music and the violin still, I can tell. It's been hard to watch it hurt you."

"I do love it," Taeva said, a pleasant ache in her chest that had nothing to do with the instrument.

What did I do to deserve such good friends?

"Where are we practicing?" Kellan asked.

Taeva scanned the room again. Two of the tables she thought were about to leave looked like they'd settled in for another round. She didn't want to subject them to the noise she was about to make. "Maybe upstairs? I'll see if my mother and Grams can cover for me since the kitchen is closed for the night."

"Perfect," Leena said, standing up. She started arranging her books in her bag, each one tucked into an exact spot so they would all fit, like a puzzle. "I'm coming too." Taeva glared at her, wide-eyed. "I won't be listening that hard. All I need is the background noise so I can get through the last bit I need to study tonight."

"Oh, alright," Taeva agreed. She made a show of rolling her eyes, but it was all to cover her nervousness. She still wasn't quite sure she wanted an audience of one, and now she had two.

Once Leena was all packed, the trio made their way toward the door to the stairs. Elawin and Grams were both behind the counter and watched Taeva and her friends approach, matching smiles on their faces.

"Can you cover for me?" Taeva asked, hating how

timidly the question came out. "Kellan is going to tutor me with some music stuff upstairs."

Elawin's happy expression didn't shift, though it looked a little forced. By contrast, Grams looked like she'd been hoping for this very thing to happen for years. But then Tirson came out of the kitchen, scowling.

"I'm going up, too. To study more," Leena added.

Tirson's entire expression changed, his eyes gleaming and full of hope. "Anything about cider in those books?"

"Not directly, but plenty of alchemy that might be useful," Leena said, playing along. "Still working on that nonalcoholic one?"

Tirson snorted. "Trying to. I'm afraid I might have to dump out the entire batch."

Taeva and Leena exchanged an awkward glance. "Surely it can't be all that bad," the wizard said.

"We'll see. You'll have to tell me if you find anything," he said.

Grams cut in. "You kids go on ahead. We've got it more than covered down here."

Taeva spun around, leading them to the door before her family could change their minds or ask too many questions. "Thank you!" she called over her shoulder.

THE GOLDMEAD LIVING ROOM WAS A PERFECT EXAMPLE OF organized chaos.

The central hearth from the tavern downstairs connected to this room, dominating the entire wall on the right side. It wasn't lit, but the warmth from the fire downstairs rose and filled the smaller room with enough heat to be comfortable. Leena deposited her books next to a worn, red plaid arm chair that Taeva was certain was older than she was. It had sat against the far wall for as long as she could remember. So had the sturdy coffee table that sat on the thick bearskin rug in the center of the room. Kellan sat his lute on the sofa that ran along the left wall. It was red plaid as well, but a slightly different pattern than the chair. They almost matched; Grams had purchased it when Taeva was a young teen and declared it close enough.

The only other furniture in the room was a tall credenza with glass doors. Inside were a few tea sets older than Grams herself, the goblet with a bee carved on it that gave the tavern its name, and—

"Is that your first violin?" Kellan asked.

Taeva joined him in front of the cabinet. "It is."

The tiny, quarter-sized instrument and its matching bow sat on the top shelf along with a brightly colored book of sheet music. It always surprised her that her parents kept the violin, even more so that they kept it on display right alongside the mead-related trinkets. She'd always felt like her father begrudged her for playing, blaming it for pulling her away from the family business.

"It's so little," Kellan said.

"I got it when I was six."

Leena plopped down in the arm chair and tucked her legs underneath her. "Very cute." Then she bent back over her studies, one book balanced between her knee and the arm of the chair and her notebook on her opposite knee.

Taeva left them for a moment and collected her violin from her room. By the time she got back, Kellan was seated on the sofa tuning his lute. He looked up when she came in, but stayed focused on his work while she took her instrument out.

Her hands were already shaking as she drew the silk

cover off her violin. Kellan or Carinthyra had tucked it safely away after she ran from the luthier shop the day before. Her fingers felt stiff and clumsy as she unbuckled the strap around the neck. She wiped her sweaty palms against her skirt, then picked it up, cramming it under her jaw with a little too much force. Taking a deep breath, she tightened the bow and drew it over the strings, tuning. Kellan didn't look up, but he plucked an A a few times for her reference.

He glanced up. "Ready?"

Taeva took another breath, shifting her feet nervously. "Yes," she answered, her voice more steady than she expected.

"We'll just waffle around in C and get a feel for it. That's all. No pressure."

"No pressure," she repeated, feeling anything but.

Her calluses had softened in the months since she'd last played, but her muscles remembered what to do. Her fingers landed on the strings with the precision born of years' worth of practice. The strings bit into them, but she ignored it. She'd built calluses before, and she could do it again. The bow bounced when it got near the frog, and she looked up nervously at Kellan.

She knew he had to have noticed her mistake, but he didn't react. He kept strumming chords at a nice slow tempo, keeping in the key of C so his playing complimented her scales. She exhaled slowly and pulled her shoulders back and down. She had to relax. She would relax.

She kept going, willing the tension in her arms and hands to ease bit by bit. Before she knew it, she was playing long, smooth bows, the notes ringing and blending with Kellan's chords. Grinning, she added a trill and was delighted that it came out bright and playful.

Kellan beamed at her. "That was nice!"

"A-hem."

Their playing lurched to a stop, and Taeva turned to see Grams in the doorway. Her grandmother grinned ear-to-ear, and to Taeva's surprise and delight, she blinked back tears.

"Sorry to interrupt, but there's an elf woman downstairs wanting to talk to you, Kellan," she said.

His brow creased. "Miralea, I bet. I wonder what she needs now." He stood up with a sigh, putting his lute on the sofa. "Want to come meet the flutist bard?"

"Absolutely," Leena said. She closed her books with two sharp snaps. "Is she single?"

Kellan gestured for Grams and Taeva to go down the stairs in front of him. "I'm not sure. You'll have to ask her yourself," he answered, huffing a laugh.

The elf flutist was waiting for them at the corner of the bar. She stood rigidly straight, scanning the tavern as one foot tapped in an irritated allegro. Her flute case was slung over one shoulder, and she carried a notebook in her other hand. She was dressed in motley that matched what Kellan wore.

"Maybe ask her on another day," Kellan said, the line reappearing between his brows. "Miralea, this is Taeva and Leena." He gestured to them both.

The bard nodded once in their direction. "Charmed," she said in a clipped tone. Even irritated, her voice was as smooth as her flute playing. Then she turned to Kellan, her gaze sharpening into a glare. "You did it again."

Kellan ran a hand through his hair, messing it up even more. "What day?"

Miralea opened her notebook and thumbed through a couple of pages before shoving it into Kellan's face. "Tomorrow! We can't be here and at Leaves at the same time."

That adorable, barely-there blush crept into Kellan's cheeks, and he glanced at Taeva. "I was going to surprise you. I asked your Grams not to tell you yet."

Taeva blushed much less glamorously than he did. "Oh," was all she could manage as she stared up at him.

Then Leena elbowed her in the ribs, and she jumped. "Still double-booking yourself? What are you going to do about it?" the wizard asked. Miralea eyed her approvingly, and Leena stood straighter, adjusting the drape of her robes.

"Easy. I'll cancel on Leaves. I've played there so many times, they won't care." He paused. "Well, they won't care that much. And I'd rather be here."

He met Taeva's eyes, and she was certain the heat in her cheeks had grown to the point that she'd become incandescent.

Miralea eyed Taeva for a long beat of silence, one brow lifted. "I see." She scored a line across the page in her book. "See you here tomorrow, then." She turned and left without another word.

"I don't think she likes me," Taeva muttered as the door closed behind the bard.

"Nonsense! That was warm for her," Kellan said with a dismissive wave. "Want to go try a different key?"

*K*ellan and Miralea arrived at the tail end of the dinner rush the following day, their drummer following silently at their heels. The bard glared at Taeva again as they walked in, her eyes piercing, like she could read all of Taeva's secrets if she looked hard enough.

It made Taeva nervous. Her anxiety had her jumping to thirty different unpleasant possibilities—from Miralea thinking she was costing them money by drawing Kellan away from the other job to the bard somehow knowing the adventurers Taeva had wronged. Maybe she knew about Taeva's violin that was tucked behind the counter and didn't approve of Kellan using his time to babysit her and her instrument.

She was chewing her bottom lip, lost in her worries and thoughtlessly cleaning the same section of the bar, when Grams popped up at her shoulder.

"He's a good-looking young man," she said, watching Kellan as he helped his drummer arrange his instruments. "And he seems nice. Can't overlook that. Looks will eventually wrinkle up and sag. A good heart stays."

"He is really kind," Taeva said. "He's been so patient with me about the violin. He has no real reason to be, but he is."

While she was grateful for it, Taeva didn't understand his calm tolerance. Her first teacher had told her if playing or performing made her nervous, she must not want it badly enough. Kellan treated her nerves like they weren't only understandable, they were *normal*. She didn't think she would ever be able to thank him enough for sitting with her in the tea shop, let alone for helping her play the night before.

"Of course he has a reason," Grams said, shaking Taeva from her reverie. "He has good taste. Any man with a brain would want an excuse to spend time with you." She looked at Taeva, her expression softening. "And he's helping you pick your violin back up. For that reason alone, I'd like him even if he looked like an ogre."

"Grams," Taeva groaned.

"Now, I know I said kissing on the first date was fine, but there's other things you'll have to be a little more careful about, like—"

"Grams! I'm twenty-two, we can skip this part. I know about—"

"Nope! I don't want to know how much you know or don't. Or why you know it, for that matter." She pointed to Taeva's violin in its case. "Just let me know when you feel up to playing some 'Up on the Riverside.' I've always loved hearing that one." She grabbed Taeva's hand and gave it a pat before walking back into the kitchen to help shut it down for the evening.

Taeva watched her go, her heart filled to bursting. Grams had always been the most supportive when it came to her music, even when Taeva started stretching into magic as well. It was so good to know that her grandmother's stance on the subject hadn't changed, even after Taeva's failure.

A traitorous voice in the back of her mind whispered that she only kept being supportive because she didn't know the whole truth of why Taeva had come home. It hissed that even Grams would look down on her if she knew Taeva had turned a dwarf into a frog, then ran off, too scared to try to put things to rights.

No, she thought, tossing her rag onto the bar and shoving the dark thoughts back into the deep hole they'd crawled out of. *I am not wasting my energy on that any more.* She was going to play later. And she was going to work on that piece for Grams. *It's in G minor, I think...*

Almost like they knew she needed a distraction, Kellan and his band started playing their first tune for the evening. They started with "The Dragon Lord's Last Stand," and over half the customers in the tavern were singing along before the first verse was even half through. Miralea wove her spells in time with the song, lighting up the entire tavern. The ribbons of magic danced through the beams in the ceiling and looped through the tables, morphing through all the colors of autumn leaves as they went. When that song was done, the band moved into another crowd favorite, then another. Patrons danced and sang with the music, laughed and twirled with the magic. And the mead flowed. Taeva, Elawin, and Grams had their hands full keeping drinks in front of their many thirsty patrons. Tirson tapped one keg after another with glee, coins glinting in his eyes. The cider stayed in the cellar, much to Taeva's relief.

Eventually, though, the band had to take a break. Kellan hopped off the stage and made straight for the bar, where Taeva poured him a mug of autumn mead.

"Thank you," he said, lifting it in a little toast to her and smiling.

"Of course," Taeva said, butterflies fluttering in her stomach. She returned to the tap to pour for Miralea and the drummer. "It's on the house. You three are putting on such a great show and drawing a big crowd. And keeping them! It's the most mead we've sold in weeks."

Kellan took another swallow and said, "You could come up and play with us."

A jolt of nervous excitement buzzed though her, leaving a tingle in her fingers. "I don't know. I'll just mess up, and then it'll throw all of you off and ruin your show."

Kellan leveled a glare at her that was part playful, part exasperated.

"And there's a lot of people in here," she confessed in a near whisper.

"We'll play something super easy so you won't mess up. And we've played these tunes so many times, we could all probably play them in our sleep. Besides, if you do happen to play something a little out of tune, no one will notice. Everyone's too drunk," he said with a shrug.

Taeva knew he was right. She served everyone in the room at least three times. The Watch would be keeping an eye on all of their patrons tonight as they swayed their way home. She looked at the stage, and that now-familiar twinge of nostalgia twisted in her chest. She'd performed on that stage countless times growing up, in front of a crowd very much like this one. And she'd been solo. Surely she could stand up there and accompany a group of skilled musicians. Add Miralea's distracting magic, and it was the perfect first step. She would be performing, but without pressure. She could keep it simple and let the others carry her.

"Alright," she said. "I'll try."

Kellan's smile brightened, and he clanked his mug down onto the bar. "Perfect. Come on, let's get you tuned up."

Taeva grabbed her violin case and followed him back to the stage, Miralea's mead in hand while Kellan carried the one for the drummer. The elf watched them approach, her eyes narrowing. Taeva gave her a weak smile as she handed her the mead. She'd been worried about playing in front of the tavern's patrons, but maybe she should have been more concerned about the bard.

Miralea took the mead without a word of thanks and cocked a brow at the case in Taeva's other hand.

"Taeva's going to play a couple tunes with us," Kellan said, picking up on the question in Miralea's look without noticing her obvious disdain.

"Is that so?" she drawled.

"One tune, that's all," Taeva said, clutching the handle of her case in both hands. "Something easy that I can play accompaniment to. As long as you don't mind."

"Of course she doesn't mind! Right, Mira?"

"Hmmm," was her only response as she sipped her mead and turned away.

That could have gone worse, I suppose, Taeva thought. She moved to the opposite side of the stage from Miralea and started prepping her violin. Her hands moved with practiced ease, with hardly a thought from her, as she tightened her bow and pulled her instrument out. Her nerves buzzed just under the surface as she tuned to the A Miralea played. She breathed through it, a steady controlled rhythm, like she had hundreds of times in the past. These were normal nerves, not the crippling anxiety that had plagued her for months.

Kellan caught her eye and winked. The heat that suffused her cheeks had nothing to do with being on stage. Why he had so much confidence in her, she had no idea, but she liked it. Probably more than she should have.

I can do this.

"Do you know 'Walking with My Love?'" Kellan asked.

Taeva nodded as she wiped her hands on her apron. It wasn't an easy piece to lead, but that would be up to

Miralea. It was in an easy key. She should be able to keep up.

Before she could decide how she would start, Kellan was counting them in, and Miralea started her short solo opening. It was slow, melodic, and her magic rose up around her in lazy spirals. Then the drummer picked up the beat, and they were off.

They played it a little quickly for a waltz, but Taeva kept up. She had the easy part—repeating a few bars across two octaves over and over through the piece—and in the past, it would have been boring. After so long of not playing, though, she found herself focusing on her fingers like they would run away if she blinked.

Just relax, just relax, just relax, she chanted to herself in time with the music. *Don't squeeze with your thumb! Dead thumb!*

She played a couple of notes out of tune and glanced up at Kellan and Miralea. The elf was ignoring her, eyes following the trails of magical light through the tavern. Kellan only nodded encouragingly, his own fingers dancing across the strings of his lute.

She kept playing, her eyes scanning over the dancers and the people still seated around tables. A few feet tapped along with the beat, but no one was booing, no one was staring at her. Maybe Kellan was right, and they were too far into their cups to notice.

The tension melted out of Taeva's shoulders. She let herself play without overthinking every movement. A feeling crept up on her, and she couldn't place it for a few bars, but ... she was having *fun.* She noticed her entire family lined up behind the bar, watching and swaying or tapping along with the beat—even her father. She smiled to herself, getting swept up in the music as surely as the dancers twirling through the magical lights on the dance floor.

Then she felt it. A familiar tingle in her fingertips that had nothing to do with the strings biting into them. The hair rose on the back of her neck, and some of the ribbons of light bobbed toward her.

Her music pulled at the magic. She hadn't meant to relax enough for something like that to happen; she didn't have enough control of it. Tension crept back in, and the notes she played took on a faint harshness. She dared a glance towards Miralea, hoping the bard hadn't noticed.

She glared at Taeva, eyes narrowed into slits. She knew. She'd felt Taeva's magic rising. Rushing toward her from the life all around them. Coming to the music's call. And she knew Taeva didn't have it under control.

Taeva tried to force her breath to steady, but it was like trying to breathe while a giant serpent tightened around her chest. She scratched out one more bar of notes before she couldn't take it anymore.

"I'm sorry," she muttered to everyone, though she wasn't sure if they could even hear her. Then she stumbled off the stage and out the back doors. If anyone called to her as she fled, she didn't hear them.

THE TINY PATIO BEHIND THE TAVERN WAS BLESSEDLY EMPTY. Taeva threw a quick prayer to every goddess she knew, thanking them for that small mercy. She wasn't sure what she would have done if people had been out back to witness her fall apart.

There wasn't much space behind The Honey Goblet, and they shared it with the florist shop behind them. The result was a somewhat cramped sitting area with two garden tables and hundreds of potted plants. Only a few things were still blooming so late in the year, but it still felt like stepping into a different, secret world. The alley narrowed into a crooked path as it passed through. It could have been mistaken for a path through an enchanted glade.

Taeva ignored all of it as she collapsed into one of the chairs, accidentally rattling the shrubby-looking plant in the middle of the table. She sat her violin in her lap and leaned her forehead against the scroll, trying to force an entire breath into her lungs.

"Taeva?" Kellan's head poked through the doors.

"Over here," she said, not bothering to pick her head up off her violin.

He pushed a particularly large leaf out of the way and spotted her. Gravel crunched as he walked up, then leaned his lute against a chair and knelt in front of her. "Are you alright?"

"No." Her voice came out whiney and pitiful, but she was too upset already to let it bother her.

"What happened? I thought you sounded great!"

She finally picked her head up, but still couldn't look him in the eye. Instead, she focused on some vines spilling out of a mead barrel-sized pot beside him. "I reached for magic while I was playing."

He perked up. "That's great! Imagine the show we could put on with two bards! If you wanted to. People would love it, though."

Taeva shook her head, closing her eyes. "I didn't mean to do it."

He was silent for a moment. "You were worried something would happen—like on your adventure."

"It could have. Easily," she admitted. She looked back toward him, certain she'd see disappointment in his face.

But there was only understanding. "It didn't, though. So you don't need to worry. Everything's fine."

He reached out and took her by the hand, bow and all. She hadn't realized how tightly she'd been squeezing it. The wood of the frog bit into her palm, and she eased her grip as he rubbed his thumb across her knuckles again.

"I wish it was that easy," she whispered.

"I know. Sometimes, even though we know in our heads that we have nothing to worry about, our hearts won't get on the same page. It means we care deeply about something. Or someone."

Kellan's eyes dropped to her lips again, and for a suspended moment, she thought he might kiss her this time. Her heart stuttered in her chest. Then his eyes closed, and he took a deep breath. Pulling back, he sat in the other chair on the opposite side of the garden table. Taeva fought to keep the disappointment off her face. She couldn't blame him, after all, for not wanting to kiss her when she was such a mess. She dropped her forehead back onto the scroll of her violin and sighed.

"Let's play something," he said in a rush. "Something that aligns with how you feel. You can let all the negativity out into the music. My first teacher taught me to do this before big performances—I sometimes still do it. I'll play backstage and imagine all the nervousness flowing out of my instrument until there's none left to carry on stage with me."

Taeva picked her head back up, intrigued. It was similar to the technique bards used to manipulate magic, which required focused visualization to bind the music and the magic together. It made sense. If imaging something hard enough would create magic, why couldn't she focus on positive things while she played and allow it to heal?

"Alright, I'll try."

Kellan pulled his lute into his lap. "Ready when you are. Just name the tune."

"How about 'My Last Coin to Lyria'?" A ballad, the song told the story of a bard who, while down on his luck, gave his last gold coin to the temple of Lyria in hopes that she would send him a song that would change his fate.

"Sounds perfect," Kellan said, placing his fingers for the first chord.

Taeva lifted her bow and hovered it over the D string. "Will you count us in?"

His eyes softened. "Absolutely." His foot tapped the gravel. "One and two and three and—"

And they played. Taeva drew her bow through the opening chord, and though she didn't think she got it perfectly in tune, she kept playing. Like Kellan suggested, she imagined all the fear and nervousness draining out of her, vibrating through the strings and up into the air, where it dissolved into nothingness. The song continued, and Taeva poured out her sadness, playing the melody that told of the bard failing even after his appeal to the goddess of song.

Then the key changed, and the melody soared as the bard finally put in the effort Lyria required and was rewarded with the perfect melody. She pulled out the last chord, adding a slow and gentle vibrato and letting it ring out a little longer than the music called for.

Taeva lowered her violin and bow slowly. Everything felt lighter, the knot in her stomach dissolved.

"Better?" Kellan asked, draping his arm over his lute.

"Better," she answered.

"Perfect."

Chapter
Seventeen

*T*aeva worked her way back through the tables to what had quickly become Leena's corner. The wizard apprentice was taking up an entire table on her own once again, books and papers covering the surface in a chaotic mess that Leena alone knew how to navigate. The lunch crowd was starting to trickle in, and she had everything laid out for another intense study session. Taeva noticed several pages of numbers and was thankful, not for the first time, that she hadn't been called to magic like the wizards were.

"Do you need anything else?" Taeva asked. Uncertain where to put it, she handed Leena a mug of autumn mead.

"This is perfect, thank you. As long as this isn't the cider, that is," she said, eyeing the drink suspiciously.

"No," Taeva said, smirking. "It's mead."

The elf shuffled a few books around to clear a space to put her drink down. "Oh, good, thank you. I'll have to thank your parents later for letting me take up so much space all the time. Especially since they insist on not taking my coin."

"If you really want to make it up to me, I have a proposition for you," Grams said, appearing at Taeva's elbow and making her jump. Again.

Taeva pressed her hand to her chest and sighed. She should be used to Grams popping up unexpectedly by now. The woman had always been a touch too sneaky.

"What do you need?" Leena asked.

Grams held out a coin purse. "Can you girls run to the market and pick up a few things? I'm almost out of some of the ingredients for my potpie, and you know how much of that we've been selling lately."

"I'd be happy to," Leena said. She shuffled around a few papers until she found a blank sheet. "What do you need?"

Taeva took the coin purse while Grams listed all the vegetables she'd need whole bushels of and a few spices they were running low on. Leena nodded along, making a list, her writing cramped and scribbled. They wouldn't be able to carry all of it back, so some of the things would have to be delivered. It was going to be an expensive trip. Taeva tucked the coin purse deep into her pocket after double-checking it for holes. She didn't want to drop a single copper. Her father would be counting every coin when they got back.

"Thanks, sugars," Grams said when she was done, then waved them on their way.

Taeva, swept up in the whole exchange, made it three steps before she gasped and turned around. "What about Leena's books?"

The wizard groaned. "I'll pack them up for now."

Grams stopped her with a dismissive wave. "They can stay right there. I'll keep an eye on them."

"You promise?" Leena said, looking at the books with a mixture of worry and longing.

"None of them will run off."

Taeva snorted and rolled her eyes, while Leena gave a brittle and forced laugh. "Alright, I'll trust you with them." Leena led the way to the door, casting a worried glance toward her books as she shrugged on a long, deep purple coat.

"Enjoy the market!" Grams called after them.

Grandhaven was having another bright and crisp autumn day. The wind that blew down the streets pushed herds of colorful leaves along with it. Hardly any foliage was left clinging to the trees, and Taeva kicked her way through knee-high drifts of gold and orange as they made their way to the market square on the south side of the city. Unlike the Grand Square, which typically hosted wares from all across Serenalyrd and the neighboring kingdoms, they were headed for a smaller square that would be full of farmers from the nearby countryside.

"Your Grams is very specific, isn't she?" Leena asked as she scanned the list again.

"She is. She'll send us right back out if we get the wrong things. But she's one of the best at what she does, so I guess she has earned the right to be picky."

"Hmm. When you put it like that, it makes me want to forgive some of the Head Wizards. There's one that even wants your desk organized a certain way." Leena shook her head, disgusted.

Taeva kicked through one last leaf pile before they crossed into the square. "Speaking of," she said, "any word from them about the clues we found?"

"Not a thing," Leena said with a sigh. "But the Head Watchman was with them when I told them what we'd discovered. He took it seriously—latched onto it all. My guess is they're busy verifying everything before they take the next step." She veered to their left without warning. "There's the carrots. We'll have to arrange for these to be delivered…"

Leena ducked into a canvas stall filled with hastily erected shelves bursting with vegetables, and Taeva followed. She picked up a few of the items Grams needed less of while Leena haggled about delivery fees, then paid for everything once Leena and the farmer reached an agreement.

"First light tomorrow morning, then," the dwarf said, taking Taeva's coin.

She suppressed a groan at the hour. It would be all hands on deck to get everything put away before the first customers trickled in. "Thank you. I'll see you then."

They stepped out of the stand, then moved to the side to review the rest of Grams' list. Leena shrugged her newly-laden pack up higher on her shoulders and glared at the paper.

"She needs a lot of fruit. For the mead? Hopefully something that'll fix the cider. Isn't it hard to find fresh fruit this time of year?"

"Yes, but there's usually a farmer here, a very rich one, who hires a wizard to keep fruit preserved for longer. It's one of the most popular stands during the fall and winter."

Leena perked up, eyes aglow. "I'd love to see what kind of spell work they use for that."

Taeva scanned the market, looking for the enchanted fruit. A few stalls down, she recognized the white rose that was emblazoned on all the wagons of the fast-moving caravan that had nearly run her over when she fled Over-hollow Fine Instruments. She'd been so vexed at the time—and frightened from coming close to being flattened—but now she felt like she could hug whoever had set such a grueling pace. Inadvertently, they'd led to her sharing her secret with Kellan. And Kellan still seemed like he wanted to be around her, by some goddess-born miracle.

The whirl of a sage green cloak caught her eye, and every muscle in her body locked tight. A tall human man with blonde hair and a short, neat beard strolled past the stands on the other side of the market. He laughed—big and booming and familiar—at something the gnome woman beside him said. The gnome was in matching sage green. And Taeva knew her too; she reached a shaking hand towards Leena's sleeve and clamped down on it like she was drowning and the other woman would keep her afloat.

Leena started, looking up from her list. "What?" Her eyes widened when she saw Taeva's stricken expression.

Taeva's pulse thudded in her ears. She ducked between two stalls, dragging Leena with her.

"What—Taeva, what's going on?" Leena whispered.

Taeva crouched behind the stall, one hand on the wood siding as she tried to force herself to take steady breaths. She attempted her normal breathing exercises, but got lost between the in-through-the-nose and the out-through-the-mouth parts.

Leena grabbed her shoulders and shook her, jarring her teeth together. "Taeva! Are we in danger?"

"No!" Taeva rushed to answer. She grabbed Leena's arms again, once more treating her like a lifeline. "Well, maybe. You aren't!"

Leena shook her again. "Breathe. In one, two, three. Out one, two, three."

Taeva followed her friend's directions, and gradually her pulse slowed and her head stopped swimming. "All right. I think I'm okay." She let go of Leena's arms and peered around the corner. The man and the gnome were nowhere to be seen.

"Good. Now explain why we had to panic and hide."

Taeva looked up at Leena, hands clasped in front of her, pleading with the half-elf to spare her this story. Leena only lifted an arched brow and waited, arms crossed.

"Fine," Taeva sighed. She hadn't planned on confessing

to Leena, but she had never planned on telling Kellan either. And if another musician didn't hate her for what she'd done, surely Leena would also understand. "I saw the adventurers I worked with back before I came home. The Sage Reavers."

She told her story again, trying to keep her voice low in case someone in the stall behind her could overhear. When she got to the part where she turned the dwarven fighter into a frog, Leena burst out laughing.

"Hush—it wasn't funny!" Taeva hissed, indignant. "It put us all in a great deal of danger!"

"But you were all fine?" Leena asked, gasping for breath.

"Um, mostly?" Taeva said with a cringe.

"Wait, did the dwarf turn back?"

"I don't know. I hope so."

"You didn't turn him back?" Leena's voice rose, and Taeva shushed her, looking over her shoulder.

"They fired me so fast, I didn't get the chance. And what if I had only made it worse?" Taeva slumped back against the stand. "Goddesses, they were so angry."

Leena stood back up, dusting off her robes. "So you're worried the reunion won't be a happy one."

"I thought, after the goblins didn't kill me, one of them would. It felt like Lyria smiled on me when all they did was fire me and leave me to wander out of the forest on my own."

"Talk about bad luck," Leena said, shaking her head and propping her fists on her hips. "I've had some spells misfire too, but never into a polymorph like that. Did burn down an outhouse once, though. Tell you what, I'll get the rest of the food. You wait here. If they were that angry, we'll play it safe."

Relief and shame churned together in the pit of Taeva's

stomach. How she'd managed to find two people who not only didn't condemn her for her mistake but actually empathized, she'd never know, but she was grateful she had. She kept expecting people to react like the adventurers had, for people to write her off and dismiss her as a lost cause. Kellan and Leena's acceptance was like a healing salve on a terrible burn.

She did feel awful, though, as she hugged her knees behind the produce stall. Clearly, she was never meant to be a bard if she couldn't even stand the thought of facing her old crew. She didn't have the courage of an adventurer. Maybe she never had.

Sighing, she hugged her knees tighter. They hadn't seen her. They would leave, and she could go back to her boring, ordinary life. Suddenly, given the choice between that and facing her old party, her normal life didn't seem so bad.

aeva was still tucked behind the stall when Leena returned, laden with two large sacks of produce. She paused for a second when she saw Taeva scrunched up on the ground, brows furrowing, but she recovered quickly.

"Up you get. I don't want to tote all this back by myself." She pulled one of the bags off her shoulder and sat it on the ground beside Taeva. "I didn't see any sage cloaks anywhere," she added, her voice going soft.

Taeva took one last shuddering breath and climbed back to her feet, brushing off her skirt. "This can't be everything," she said, forcing some levity into her voice.

Leena snorted. "Not even half. You saw that list! Most of it will be delivered in the morning."

Taeva scooped up her half of the load, and they set off, wandering back through the leaf-covered streets. Leena kept up a steady stream of chatter, sharing bits of gossip she'd picked up in the market as they went. A wave of gratitude engulfed Taeva as Leena laughed at her own story. How many other people would have come back to find her curled up on the verge of panic and *not* made a fuss? If Leena had sat with her and tried to comfort her, she would have dissolved into tears. The half-elf seemed to have known that and opted to act like nothing strange was happening instead.

It was exactly what Taeva had needed. She didn't know

how she'd found such a good friend, but surely it was a gift from Lyria that Leena had wandered into the tavern.

"We're taking a quick detour. Come on," Leena said. She grabbed Taeva's elbow and pulled her onto a cross street that ran north towards the Grand Square.

"To where?" Taeva asked, confused.

"Moslock Potions," the wizard answered brightly.

"Oh, something for school?"

Leena hesitated, then gave an off-handed shrug. "Kind of? I want to apprentice with the owner—Quinn Moslock—eventually, so any excuse for me to be in there is a good excuse..."

She trailed off, and Taeva could hear the "but" her friend wasn't saying. "And?" she prompted.

Leena looked away guiltily. "And I want to ask about Amberwood's poison."

Taeva stopped walking for a second, stunned, then had to jog to catch back up. She grabbed Leena and pulled her to a stop at under one of the nearly-bare trees.

"You don't think that's a bad idea? What if the person, or people, that killed him find out we've been asking around?" Taeva whispered.

"They won't," Leena said. "Alchemists never share their customers' business. He won't tell anyone what we ask about."

"You hope! And we aren't even customers!"

"He won't. If he did and anyone found out, he'd be ruined. Alchemists are sworn to secrecy." She started walking again, striding stubbornly ahead. "Trust me! It'll be fine."

"If he can't share anything, what's the point?" Taeva said, scurrying to keep up with Leena's longer strides.

"Just come on!"

Moslock Potions was only two streets away from the Grand Square. Given the location, Taeva was expecting someplace grand, like where they'd bought their dresses for the ball. Instead, the alchemist's shop was a narrow slice of a store wedged between a cobbler and a hatter. With its darkened windowpanes and the plain sign hanging over the door—just a rectangle reading *Potions*—it looked like it belonged in a shadier part of the city. Leena opened the door—there was no merry bell chime to signal their entrance—and Taeva followed her in, shoulders inching up to her ears as her feelings of apprehension grew.

A counter ran along the right wall and across the back of the shop, but the rest of the space was filled with shelves. Potion bottles, boxes of bones, and jars with unidentifiable things floating around inside filled every available space until the shelves seemed to lean in toward each other. The darkened windows fought against letting in any sunlight, and the lanterns that flickered in the corners cast more shadows than light. An acrid smell hung in the air, and Taeva wrinkled her nose, frowning.

She drew closer to Leena. "You *want* to apprentice here?"

"Hello, hello!" a voice called from the counter before Leena could answer. "A moment, please!"

An aging gnome worked at the counter near the corner, pouring wax over the top of a bottle to seal it. His grey hair sprang up from his head in all directions, the locks on the left singed and crinkled. The spectacles that perched on his nose were even thicker than the bottle he was sealing. When he looked up as they approached, he looked more like a burnt owl than a gnome.

"Ah, an apprentice from the Academy. Lara, was it?" he asked, taking in Leena's robes.

One of Leena's brows twitched, but her voice was still

pleasant when she answered. "Leena. And this is my friend, Taeva. Taeva, this is Quinn Moslock, master alchemist."

"Hm, a bard! What interesting company," Quinn said, adjusting his spectacles.

The word hit Taeva like a lightning bolt. *How in the name of Lyria does he know?* She forced a smile and counted her breaths, willing her heart to slow. He wasn't going to ask her for a magical demonstration. Everything would be fine.

"What can I do for the two of you?"

"I have some questions for you, if you have time," Leena said.

"I always have time for students of the Academy! What have you been pondering?"

"Is there a way to make oils or potions stay on sword blades?" Her tone was casual, but Taeva recognized the glint in the half-elf's eyes. It was the same one she had when she was hunting for answers in her text books. A hound on the scent.

"You absolutely can. But," Quinn answered, pointing a finger matter-of-factly, "it takes a very clever combination of ingredients and magic to get them to stay on the metal for any length of time. Without it, the potion will eventually run off the blade and make a mess in the scabbard."

"And you know the correct combination?" Leena asked.

"Of course! *Master* alchemist, remember? I make an oil for a butcher's cleavers and knives so they never dull. A fire tonic for a tanner, so his edges burnish themselves as he cuts. And that *stuff* I made for that late fellow," he said, trailing off.

"You made Amberwood's poison?" Taeva blurted out before she could stop herself.

Quinn started clearing off the counter, and his voice took on a haughty tone. "I hadn't realized his poison affinity had become common knowledge." It was more misdirection than answer.

"He was killed," Leena pointed out. "You aren't oath-bound to keep his secrets any more."

The alchemist pulled out a damp cloth and started wiping down the scarred surface of the counter. "I suppose you're right," he said with a sigh. "Yes, yes, I made his poison. I didn't love the idea, mind you, but I did it. I wish it could have saved Amberwood in the end. It would have if he'd listened to me."

"What do you mean?" Taeva asked.

"He wanted a slow-acting poison so people could be saved. Something that would make people slow and sick but would have obvious signs so they wouldn't escape notice when they sought treatment. I think it was part of his bid for taking over the Watch—a more humane way of incapaci-tating criminals, I suppose. Make them ill so they have to turn themselves in instead of maiming or killing them. I told him if you've already drawn your sword, it's time for swift justice." He mimed swinging a sword, tipping precariously to the side as he did. "Fight so you yourself can see the next day! I told him he wanted something fast-acting. But he refused. So, I made him the distilled basilisk poison."

Taeva and Leena looked at each other. Taeva was almost certain they were both thinking about Silversage leaving a different apothecary, tucking something secret into his coat.

"Is that antidote easy to come by?" Taeva asked.

"It is. That was part of what he wanted. It leaves an easily identifiable wound—turns all the veins around it green and nasty. Makes the target sick and weak, gradually worsening until they're bedridden. But the antidote is just a mixture of common herbs with the twist of a very simple spell. It takes several doses over a long period to neutralize the poison, but anyone could make it."

Taeva hadn't seen any wounds on Silversage, but then again, it was autumn. Anyone could be hiding poisoned wounds under their coats and cloaks. Moslock Potions was closer to the Silversage home, too. Why would he have gone to an apothecary on the other side of the city unless he'd been trying to avoid tipping off the same person who'd made the poison? All Quinn would have to do then would be to refuse Silversage's business and report him.

Taeva's mind whirled as Leena said her goodbyes. All arrows kept pointing toward Silversage. She was fairly certain they'd solved the case. All that was left to do was wait for the Head Wizards to agree and bring it before the king and council. Hopefully they would hurry before anyone else fell to Silversage's ambitious blade.

he entire Goldmead family was up early the next morning, ready to receive the delivery from the produce stands they'd patronized the day before. Taeva stoked the fire in their big open hearth, chasing the chill out of the room. By the time she threw open the curtains and the front door, the delivery driver was making his way down their street, a cart bumping over the cobbles behind him.

"Morning!" he called.

Taeva stifled a yawn with the back of her hand, then said, "Good morn—"

Miralea appeared from behind the cart like she'd materialized there.

The bard looked like she was ready to conquer the stage, even though she wasn't in her usual motley. She wore cream breeches with a blue tunic and tall leather boots up to her knees. A long black coat billowed behind her as she made a direct path toward The Honey Goblet.

Taeva's heart sank. Miralea looked like a real adventurer dressed like that. Her eyes keen, her strides confident.

"I need to speak with you," she said as she drew up even with the cart as it parked in the street outside the tavern's front door.

She sounded too stern and serious for this to be a casual social call. *She's come to scold me about distracting Kellan and wasting his time with lessons,* Taeva thought as she gestured to the produce cart. "It'll be a little while, I can't keep this gentleman waiting." Hopefully, if they worked slow, Miralea would get tired of waiting and just leave.

"Don't be ridiculous!" Grams said, bustling through the door with Tirson. "We handled this while you were off on your little adventure, we can handle it now. Talk to your friend."

Miralea's gaze narrowed as Grams spoke, and Taeva felt the blood drain from her face. She was pinned between the proverbial rock and hard place—her Grams and the tetchy bard. Miralea gestured to the corner of the tavern, and Taeva reluctantly followed her over, hugging herself against the morning chill.

Once they were out of earshot, Miralea rounded on her with a dagger-sharp glare. "You are a bard," she accused.

Taeva froze. Of all the possible routes this conversation could have taken, this was the one she was least prepared for. After her mistake with the magic, Miralea had ignored her like normal, so Taeva thought she must not have noticed after all. It turned out that she couldn't have been more wrong. "I— I... I don't know what you mean," she stumbled out.

Miralea cocked her head and narrowed her eyes even further, incredulous. "Don't lie to me like that. I was a wizard even before I was a bard, and I have been a bard for a long time. I know what I saw."

"What did you see?" Taeva asked, breathless. She was afraid she already knew the answer.

"You pulled on my magic while you were playing with us the other night. It split away from me so easily it was like I wasn't even holding it."

Taeva looked at the ground. "I didn't mean to."

"Didn't *mean to?*"

"I've never been very good at controlling it. I tried to! I had a teacher, and I studied for a long time. I thought I had it under control, or at least well enough in hand, but then..." She trailed off, looking back up to meet Miralea's piercing gaze. "I didn't after all. So I quit."

Something softened around the edges of Miralea's expression for a heartbeat. If Taeva hadn't been looking at her, she would have missed it. "What happened?" the bard asked.

Never in a million years would Taeva share her whole story with Miralea. She rubbed her arms, trying to bring some warmth back into them, and settled for an abridged version. "I lost control of the magic while on a job with an adventuring crew. No one was hurt, not badly, but it was a close call. Too close. So I came back home."

Miralea crossed her arms and studied her for a moment, her focus so intense Taeva could have sworn the elf was looking at her thoughts, not her face. "You were the one who turned Mert into a frog, weren't you?"

Taeva had to take a step back to steady herself as the ground was snatched from beneath her feet. "What?" she whispered, unable to get any other words out.

"You were the bard Heathric hired. The Sage Reavers."

Taeva thought briefly about running away, but stuffed most of her fear into the dark corner where she normally kept it. After all, where would she go? If she wanted to, Miralea could use her magic to tie Taeva's feet in place. She had no doubt the bard's flute was tucked inside her coat. And did she even need it? She was a wizard too. Taeva didn't stand a chance.

"I was," she answered, her voice barely above a whisper. She looked away again, unable to meet Miralea's gaze.

The elf was silent for a moment. Taeva could feel her

gaze on her, though. She was being studied again, under a new, more unforgiving light. It made the back of her neck prickle. She was suddenly glad she'd confessed to Kellan already. If the story had reached him from Miralea's lips, she was certain it would have been twisted to paint her in an even less flattering light.

"They aren't out for vengeance, you know," Miralea said.

"They aren't?" She looked back to the bard, eyes wide.

Miralea shook her head. "Not at all. I know them. I've worked with them. They were furious, don't get me wrong. Especially Mert. But they were able to hire a wizard to reverse the spell and turn him back. Thankfully, it didn't revert on its own while he was in Lily's pocket."

Taeva sagged with relief. "I was so worried he was stuck that way. They fired me before I could try to change him back. Of course I might have made it worse…"

"They shouldn't have done that. I told them as soon as I heard the story."

"Do you know them well?"

"Yes. I've worked with them many times over the years. They're in the city right now, you know."

"I saw Heathric and Lily yesterday," Taeva answered. "I hid from them." The admission made her feel tiny and vulnerable.

Miralea didn't take advantage, though, much to Taeva's relief. "Don't be shocked if they come to apologize. I've told them they should. You made a huge mistake." Taeva flinched. "But so did they."

"I know. I don't blame them. It's why I gave up magic. Music, too, until recently."

Miralea's brow creased, and she frowned—the most expression Taeva had ever seen on her face. "Don't be ridiculous." She sounded angry. Even more so than when she showed up to scold Kellan about his schedule.

Taeva backpedaled. "I didn't... I don't—"

The bard poked her in the forehead, and she reeled back, shocked.

"There's too much ability stored in that brain for you to waste it," Miralea said, her expression dark.

Taeva blinked at her for a moment. The comment sounded almost like a compliment. Then she gave herself a good mental shake. It didn't matter how much magic Miralea thought she could wield if she wasn't able to control it. She was a danger to herself and those around her—more so if she wielded more potent magic.

"It doesn't matter," she muttered. "I can't control it."

Miralea scoffed, putting her hands on her hips. "You do too much. Do less."

Taeva tilted her head. "What?"

"The magic will respond to even a simple scale. Meanwhile, from what the Reavers told me, you were always trying to shape it with complex pieces."

"It's what I was taught," Taeva said, her confusion plain in her tone. "Complex magics need complex music to contain them."

"Horse shit," Miralea said, throwing a hand in the air. "Clearly, your teacher was never in battle. Keep it simple. The simpler, the better. Your mind and the link it forms between the music and the magic are what's important, not the collection of notes you use to form that link."

Taeva stood rooted in place, her mind reeling. "It can't be that easy."

"It both is and isn't, like anything with magic. But try it." Miralea looked at the sun and sighed. "Enough life advice.

I'm due at the Silversage home. Again." She rolled her eyes and turned to leave.

"Silversage?" Taeva said, perking up. "This early?"

"Unfortunately. He's hired me so often over the last few months he might as well put me on permanent salary. Always asking me to conjure an illusory opponent for him to spare with. Right-handed, left-handed, prone, everything. He's paid me a pretty bit of coin, but I'm cheaper and more available than anyone at the Wizard's Academy, aren't I?"

Taeva nodded dumbly. She was only half listening, her mind instead replaying Silversage's comment about being glad Amberwood was dead and then him storming out of the apothecary.

Miralea turned and started sauntering away, then called over her shoulder, "See you soon. Don't get in too much trouble."

And then she walked away without another backward glance. Taeva watched her go, trying to absorb the entirety of what just happened.

They were right about Silversage. All his training with Miralea's illusions must have given him the skill to cut down Amberwood and his guards. She hoped the Head Wizards took her and Leena's information seriously.

Tucking an errant curl behind her ear, Taeva turned to help with the last of the produce. She replayed the rest of Miralea's visit as she carried celery inside, going over each point until the conversation was worn smooth like river rock.

Mert wasn't still trapped as a frog. That alone changed her entire outlook on her misadventure. Pair it with the Sage Reavers not being out for revenge, and the sense of relief could have melted her into a puddle in the street. It was a far cry from forgiveness, but knowing she didn't need to fear them anymore lifted so much weight off her shoulders it was staggering. She hadn't realized how much it had worn her down. Perhaps that was the danger in carrying something alone for so long. A person could grow accustomed to the weight, even as it bent them.

And the information about magic had her picking at the fresh calluses on her fingers nervously as she waited for customers to start wandering in. She was so tempted to try something simple. She could play a short tune to help light the fires and heat the stove and oven in the kitchen, like Leena had. She could even try her hand at dancing lights like Miralea—nothing *useful* by some people's standards, but it certainly brought joy to a lot of people. Surely, if it made people happy, it was its own kind of useful. Just like music itself.

Music first, she told herself. *And if that keeps going well ... maybe a little bit of magic. Maybe.*

Chapter Twenty

The lull between lunch and dinner dragged on, and the tavern was mostly empty. Two Watchmen sat at the bar talking to Tirson about his plans for the winter mead, but they were the only patrons in the building. Outside, it was gloomy and overcast, the wind sharp with the promise of winter's bite. Inside, though, the fire roared in the hearth, warming the entire room and casting it all in a golden orange glow.

Taeva and Kellan sat on the edge of the stage, their feet dangling off the side. Extra warmth flushed in Taeva's cheeks as Kellan leaned over, lute in his lap, and nudged her with his shoulder.

"Take the lead when I get back around the C chord," he half-chanted to the rhythm of the jig they were playing.

She gave the tiniest of nods, her violin tucked under her jaw. He reached the C, and she took a deep breath, then flew. Her fingers danced over the strings as she took over the melody. The jig was fast, and she kept her fingers and wrists loose, moving back and forth between the strings without bouncing or squeaking. Kellan's foot started tapping beside her, and a smile grew on both of their faces.

It sounded good. Great, even.

Her fingertips tingled as magic rose to her music's call. She held her breath and quickly shoved it from her mind, but the distraction cost her. The next two notes were a little out of tune, the timing a little off. She winced, glancing at Kellan. She knew he noticed. There was no way a musician like him would miss that.

But his grin was still in place, his foot still tapping. "There you go. Just play right through it," he said. "We only noticed because we've studied it. Most people don't listen that hard."

She did what he said, playing through the rest of the piece. The magic rose once more, and she had to shove it into the corner of her mind, but she recovered more quickly, only playing one note a little sharp. When she played the last note—a long sustained G that she couldn't resist adding some vibrato to—she was grinning like a fool again.

The Watchmen at the bar gave them a scattered round of applause as they made their way out the door. Taeva's smile grew until her cheeks hurt. She bobbed a quick half-bow at them.

"Keep it up, honey," her father said as he rounded the corner into the kitchen, leaving them alone in the main room. Taeva's heart swelled until it squeezed against her ribs.

"That was great! No playing for months, and then busting that out in a few days. I should hire you," Kellan said.

The thought could have warmed Taeva all on its own in the dead of winter. "I don't think Miralea would like that very much," she said, half-way teasing. Miralea might tolerate it, but she was certain the elf wouldn't enjoy it.

"Sure she would," Kellan said. "She likes you! And when she hears you play again, with all your new confidence, she'll agree. Some fiddle would be the feather in our cap, you know?"

Taeva grinned but shook her head. "I don't think she likes me at all."

Kellan propped his lute against the stage and leaned back on his left hand—the one closest to Taeva. His expression grew serious as he studied her face. "She does like you. But even if she didn't, it doesn't matter. *I* like you. A lot, actually."

His gaze fell to her lips, and she suddenly forgot how to breathe.

"You do?" she managed to whisper.

"I do."

He leaned forward, and Taeva's heart squeezed so tight she thought it might have stopped beating. Her eyes fluttered closed.

The front door swung open, and they jumped apart, a muttered curse on Kellan's lips. Taeva pressed a hand to her chest; her heart pounded against it like a caged animal.

Their intruder was Leena, and she stormed over the moment she saw them, purple robes billowing in her wake. Taeva hoped the half-elf hadn't seen what she'd interrupted, but judging by the thunderous look on her face, she didn't have to worry.

Leena grabbed an empty chair and dragged it closer to the stage, then turned it backwards and straddled it, resting her arms on the back as she glared at Taeva and Kellan.

"They arrested him," she spat.

It took Taeva a moment to catch up with Leena's train of thought, but then she straightened, eyes opening wider. "Silversage?"

"Yes," Leena said, glaring.

Taeva hesitated, not quite understanding her friend's anger. "But that's good ... right? Case closed. Murderer off the streets."

Leena sighed, her anger evaporating as she melted over the back of the chair. "Yes, it's great. But they aren't giving us any credit," she whined.

Taeva glanced at Kellan and fought to keep from laughing. "I'm sure they did some of their own investigating," he said.

"That's the thing—I don't think they did! The Head Wizards have all been present for all their lectures; their office hours haven't been interrupted. Things have been business as usual ever since the king released them from their investigating duties."

That made Taeva uneasy. "But what we have is mostly circumstantial," she argued.

"It was more than what they had otherwise," Leena said. "Think about it." Leena rattled off the information they had, counting their clues on her fingers. "We know Amberwood carried poisoned blades, and the killer was injured and, therefore, poisoned. Silversage was very open that he was glad Amberwood was dead—"

"And they argued in front of Amberwood's staff," Taeva added.

Leena pointed to her. "Exactly. Then you two saw Silversage leaving the apothecary, possibly getting an antidote for the poison. Taeva and I found out it was distilled basilisk poison, which is slow-acting. So he would have had time to get an antidote, and he would have needed multiple doses."

"And injuries caused by a left-handed fighter," Taeva muttered, remembering what the Watchmen had told her shortly after the murders.

Kellan cocked his head, frowning. "Left-handed? Silversage isn't left-handed."

Leena lowered her fingers and gripped the back of the

chair tight enough for her knuckles to turn white. "How do you know?"

Kellan shrugged a single shoulder. "I've worked there a lot. I've always noticed when people are left-handed, I guess because it makes me think about how different their learning process with the lute would be. It's interesting. Anyway, I've only seen Silversage do things right-handed."

"Well. That's a problem," Leena said, leaning back.

Taeva shook her head. "I talked to Miralea this morning. She said Silversage has been hiring her to conjure a sparing illusion for him. She said he practices with both hands."

"So it really was him," Leena mused. "We solved the murderous plot even the Watchmen couldn't untangle."

"I can't believe it," Kellan said. "I worked there so many times and never thought he was ruthless enough for something like that. Cunning? Yes. Cold sometimes? Absolutely." He rubbed a hand over his face. "I even played there after he killed Amberwood in cold blood."

He looked stricken, like by taking jobs for the killer-lord, he had somehow helped commit the crime himself. Taeva reached over and took his hand, like he'd done for her so many times.

"You didn't know. You did nothing wrong," she said, giving his hand a squeeze.

He turned their hands over so he could brush his thumb across her knuckles. Leena looked at their hands, a mischievous smirk spreading across her face. Maybe she had seen their near-kiss after all.

A blush burned across Taeva's cheeks. Again.

Chapter
Twenty-One

The postman wandered out of the tavern, one of Grams' biscuits already half eaten in his hand. Taeva watched him go, holding another letter addressed to her, written in a hand that was quickly becoming as familiar to her as her own. It'd been two days since she'd seen Kellan, and he'd written her both days. Thinking of him waking up early to write her each morning before the post was collected made her chest ache in the sweetest way.

The day before, he'd written:

Taeva,

I'll be stuck at jobs all the way on the other side of Grandhaven today. If I were closer, I'd come by to see you during every break. Knowing I won't have the chance is going to make this day take forever.

Thinking of you,
Kellan

She dropped off the rest of the mail in the kitchen, then scurried back behind the counter to open his latest letter.

. . .

Taeva,

I pulled some strings (Miralea wasn't happy, but she'll live) and will come by as soon as I can. I hope you're available. And that I'm not assuming too much.

I can't wait to see you.

Kellan

She squished the letter to her chest, feeling every bit like a love-struck heroine from one of her novels. Seeing him later would be the highlight of her day—hopefully it would be sooner rather than later. She pulled the letter away from herself and read it again, smiling. It sounded like he was supposed to have been busy today. Miralea not being happy was also likely an understatement.

Hopefully she and Kellan would have time to play again, though if he was only popping in for a visit between gigs, it might not be possible. She'd been practicing on her own since the last time they played, trying to learn some of the pieces she'd heard Kellan and Miralea playing. It felt good to work on memorizing music again. Like stretching a muscle that hadn't been used for a while, but also like putting on an old favorite dress.

Hopefully, and she was scared to admit it to herself, let alone out loud, she could perform with Kellan and Miralea again. She felt like Kellan would agree to it, but even after Miralea's round-about about encouragement, she couldn't help but feel like she annoyed the bard every time they interacted. But they both played so well, and Taeva was familiar with their music choices. It was a small risk. Still a bit of a gamble, but the one with the best odds.

The magic, of course, was the biggest threat. Over the

past couple of days, it had risen to the call of her music multiple times, even though she wasn't reaching for it. She kept pushing it down, blocking it from her mind, and even that was getting easier. She'd done it so many times now that she could lock it away without missing a single beat and while easily keeping in tune. After her conversation with Miralea, it made her feel an odd twinge of guilt, like she was caging herself. But if it kept everyone safe, she'd keep the door locked tight, no matter how much it made her heart ache.

She refolded the letter and was tucking it into the pocket of her apron when Leena walked in, bowed under the weight of her books like normal.

"Another study day?" Taeva asked brightly.

"Yes," Leena said, dragging out the word as she made her way to her usual table. "And it's a good thing, too. We're still working on evocation, but it is *not* getting any easier. Ice and fire? Who can really do that well?" She dropped her bag on the table with a resounding thud.

"I certainly can't," Taeva answered. She took a stack of books from Leena and moved them to the far end of the table. "Have you been able to read any of *The Blackdawn Curse*?"

Leena's eyes lit up, and she paused in her unpacking. "I have! How far have you gotten? I don't want to ruin anything."

"Chapter fifteen."

The wizard leaned across the table, eyes glowing with excitement. "So you met the dragon!"

"I love the dragon," Taeva said, squeezing the books she held without realizing it. "She's so snarky."

"What about Blackdawn? How do you feel about him?"

They resumed unpacking while they discussed the

novel, Leena giving occasional directions on where to stack her school books. The front door opened again, letting in a gust of chilly autumn air that could be felt all the way in Leena's back corner. Kellan strode in, dressed in the solid grey outfit he'd worn when Taeva first met him, lute in its case across his back. His gaze swept over the bar then landed on them in the corner, and he smiled bright enough to light up the entire room. Taeva's stomach flipped somersaults as she waved him over.

"Ladies," he said, dropping into an exaggerated bow. He stood back up, his focus purely on Taeva. "Fancy meeting you here."

Leena rolled her eyes. "Sap."

Taeva gave her arm a light smack. "On your way to perform?" she asked Kellan.

"Yep, back at the little square with the fountain. I wanted to see you first, though." He produced a single white rose from behind his back and offered it to her. As Taeva took it, his fingers brushed across hers in a way she was certain was deliberate. "Since you're both here, though, did you hear the news?"

"News?" Leena asked, looking up from arranging the last of her book piles. The table was completely covered once again.

"They held Silversage's trial yesterday. It sounds like it was a messy, rushed affair—no witnesses or anything. They didn't even assemble a true jury. The king just sat in to declare the verdict."

Taeva had never watched any court proceedings, but she'd read enough to know that there was usually so much to plan that even setting a date for a trial took longer than a few days.

"Rushed? That goes against the decrees set by the first

Dragonsbane," Leena said. "No wonder they gave us a study day today. All the Head Wizards must be in court."

Kellan shook his head. "If they are, it's for something else. The trial is over. The king himself declared Silversage guilty."

Taeva and Leena exchanged a stunned look.

"They gave him a week to get his affairs in order. Then he's going to be executed—beheaded."

KELLAN LEFT IN A RUSH TO MAKE IT TO HIS GIG, LEAVING Taeva and Leena alone with the wizard's books again. Taeva stared at the door with her brows furrowed. She was glad that Silversage had been found guilty and wouldn't be able to continue plotting against the other nobles—especially since he had no qualms about maiming innocent guards if they happened to step between him and his goals. It even filled her with a certain degree of pride that it had been her and her friends who'd helped make sure his scheming came to an end.

But something about the rushed nature of the trial and sentencing nagged at her. She adjusted a few of Leena's books, imaging Grams throwing profane insults at the king and the nobles. She'd likely put it all down as the king trying to save face and make the rest of the nobility feel safe again. There was probably some truth in that, but Taeva still couldn't shake the feeling that there was something else going on.

There was something she was missing, but she couldn't quite pin it down.

Leena was starting to settle in behind her fortress of

books when Tirson came out of the kitchen, a bottle of cider in hand.

"Alright, girls. Let's try this one more time," he said, grabbing a pair of glasses from behind the bar. "I added some sugar back to the cider now that it's done aging, so hopefully that fixes our bitterness problem."

Taeva glanced at Leena. The half-elf dragged herself back out of her chair, fixing a polite smile across her face. "Not loud enough yet anyway..." she muttered.

Taeva bit back a laugh as they joined her father at the bar. He poured a finger of cider into a glass for each of them, then one for himself. The cider was cloudier than when they'd last taste-tested it, and Taeva eyed it suspiciously while Tirson corked the bottle.

"Bottoms up!" he said.

All together, they lifted their glasses and took sips. Taeva grimaced and set her glass back on the bar, unfinished. It wasn't bitter anymore, that was for sure. Instead, it didn't taste like a cider at all. It was all sugar, with hardly a hint of apple or cinnamon in the mix.

Tirson threw the entirety of his sample back, then all but slammed his glass onto the counter with a sneer. "Did the two of you hate that as much as I did?" he asked.

Leena scooted her glass back across the bar, half the cider still sloshing around in it. "I didn't love it."

"I thought I had it that time," Tirson said, scrubbing a hand through his greying blonde hair. "This is the first batch of drink that I've ever ruined."

"Batch?" Taeva asked, eyes going wide. "You added that much sugar to the entire batch?"

"Yes, honey, I did. Goddesses, your Grams is never going to let me hear the end of this." He glared at the murky cider in the bottle.

Leena locked eyes with Taeva, lifted her brow, then jerked her chin at something against the back wall. Taeva looked over to where her friend was indicating. Her violin case was tucked behind the bar.

"Oh," Taeva said, her palms already getting sweaty.

"Can you do it?" Leena asked.

Taeva hesitated. She'd done very simple transformation spells while she was studying under her bard teacher. This time last year, she wouldn't have hesitated to try magicking the cider. But in the aftermath of her magical catastrophe, she worried she'd burn the entire tavern down.

Her conversation with Miralea came to mind. The elf had said magic didn't require the music to be complex. She could play a scale, and as long as her focus was good and her intention was clear, there was no reason she couldn't work any number of spells.

E minor, she thought. The notes popped into her mind so clearly it was like Lyria herself had placed them there. So many jigs were in that key. And what went better with meads and ciders than a jig?

"I have an idea," she announced, already moving to grab her violin.

"Hm?" Tirson turned away from the bottle, his expression lighting up.

"It might not work—"

"It will," Leena cut in.

"—but I'd like to try."

Tirson was silent as Taeva picked up her case and placed it on the bar. Her hands shook as she reached for her bow, taking it out of the slot in the lid. She ignored her own trembling, focusing on her breathing and on tightening the bow hair.

"Leena, will you come down too? Just in case?"

The wizard's expression was soft, but she answered with a flippant, "You won't need me, but sure."

By the time Taeva pulled her violin out, Tirson was rocking back and forth on the balls of his feet, grinning.

"This is going to save us so much on supplies," he said. Taeva could almost see the numbers whirling through his head. "Not only saving, though, the lunch crowd will be lining up down the street all season!"

Taeva latched onto the distraction, thinking about all the extra work that would bring instead of on what she was about to try. Maybe they'd finally have to hire help. She shook herself and pushed the thought aside. With a death grip on the neck of her fiddle, she motioned for her father to lead the way.

The usually-neat cellar was a disaster. The keg of cider was pulled into the middle of the room, its lid pried off and discarded in the middle of the floor. Notebooks and loose sheets of paper lay scattered all across the bar-height tables, some having fluttered onto the floor. Tirson waded through and over them, unconcerned.

He'd kept up a string of increasingly hyperbolic hopes regarding the success of the cider the entire walk down the stairs. He stopped in front of the keg and added, "But don't put extra pressure on yourself, honey. Fixing a mistake this large might be beyond the Head Wizards themselves." He toed the keg, scowling.

"She has it under control," Leena said, giving Taeva another reassuring smile.

Taeva's heart beat so hard it ached. "Stand back, please," she said, bringing her violin up to her shoulder.

Leena and Tirson stepped back against the bookshelf,

the former rolling up her sleeves and flexing her fingers. Having her friend ready to counter any mistake she made lent Taeva a smidgeon of confidence. At least any damage she might cause would be contained.

She lifted her bow. She'd start the scale on an open string. It was technically wrong, but all she would have to do was bow; no left hand required. She took a deep breath, focused on the cider, and played.

One long, smooth bow after another. She played as calmly as she could, thinking about the taste of the cider matching the notes, sweet like the joy on people's faces while they danced to a jig. She kept the tasting notes in mind, letting her fingers go through the scale she'd played hundreds of times before. It was second nature.

The magic rose to her call, tingling in her fingertips. Her knee-jerk reaction was to fight against it again, but she closed her eyes and let it flow through her, willing her muscles to loosen and keeping her focus on the cider and what she wanted it to become. Light bloomed in her instrument, bright even against her closed lids, then slowly faded away as she played the final E in the scale.

She cracked an eye open as she lowered her instrument. "No fire," she whispered.

Leena scoffed. "Of course there isn't. It did glow in a pretty way, though."

Taeva held her bow and violin in one hand and peered into the keg. The murkiness had vanished from the cider, leaving it a clear golden color. "Looks pretty," she murmured.

"Time for another taste test!" Tirson proclaimed.

He took three glasses down from the rack and poured a little cider into each with a twist of the tap. Taeva watched the entire procedure with a lump in her throat. She hadn't caught their home on fire, but she still might have turned the cider into poison. Or maybe it would turn them all into frogs. The thought would have made her laugh if she hadn't been so nervous.

Her father passed her drink over, and she sniffed at it. It smelled normal—bright like a crisp apple, with a hint of cinnamon and sweetness. She even twirled it in the glass. Nothing out of the ordinary happened. No explosions. No swirls of malevolent color.

"Goddesses," Leena said.

Taeva's heart skipped a beat. "What is it?"

"It's delightful!"

Tirson hummed in appreciation. "It is!"

They both tipped their glasses back and drained the rest of their samples without hesitation. Hope sparked to life in Taeva's chest as she watched. Then she lifted her own glass and took a swig.

It tasted like it smelled. Ripe apple burst across her tongue, followed by a mix of cinnamon and sugar that could stand toe-to-toe with her Grams' best pies. She sat the glass down on the closest table, stunned.

"I did it," she said.

Tirson beamed at her, pride in every line of his face. "You did!" He put an arm around her shoulders and gave her a squeeze. "I knew you could. My daughter. Musical and mead-ical genius."

Taeva and Leena both snorted, then dissolved into a fit of giggles. Tirson chuckled as he got to work bottling more of the cider. Free samples would be passed around tonight, Taeva knew. And she fully expected it to be a sweeping success.

She took another sip of the cider, unable to keep the smile off her lips. It was the first drink she'd helped create.

All her time in The Honey Goblet, and she'd never so much as discussed ingredients for a new mead.

And now she'd made this one with magic. Maybe adventuring like the great bards in her books wasn't for her, but so many other possibilities had opened up. And they were just a bow-stroke away.

*A*fter they made their way back to the main floor of the tavern and Leena returned to her studies, patrons started flooding in. News of the trial and its speedy turn around was all anyone could talk about.

It drove all thoughts of cider straight from Taeva's mind. She asked a few strategic questions, trying to see how people felt about the case, and got nearly the same answer from all of them. The people were relieved. They didn't have to worry about a killer being on the loose, and they were glad to have a corrupt aristocrat ousted. Something about it still niggled in the back of Taeva's mind, though, like a splinter. Shouldn't there have been more of an investigation? The king was basing his judgment on information that had come from a barmaid, a lutist, and a student. Taeva knew she and her friends weren't fools, but surely professionals should have looked for more substantial evidence.

The clues they'd found had certainly been damning, but the rushed manner of the trial also nagged at her. Everyone deserved to bring evidence to their own defense, just in case the investigation had looked at things from the wrong angle. Silversage hadn't had that option.

The thought weighed on her throughout the rest of the day, growing more insistent as the hours stretched on. Watchmen came in, and other patrons bought them drinks. Toasts were lifted in honor of Head Watchmen Tybrecht, and more rounds were ordered. It was the busiest day they'd had since the flood of people after the memorial for Amberwood. By the time the dinner crowd died down to the last few stragglers, Taeva's feet ached from running back and forth through the tables without rest. She collapsed onto her stool behind the counter, Grams on her cushioned one right beside her.

"What a day!" Grams said, cracking open the lid to the coin box. "Nothing like a bit of good news to get people to spend their coin."

"Do you think he really did it?" Taeva asked. "The trial..."

"Found him guilty, didn't it? Silversage always seemed like he was up to no good anyway. Never did like him. He screwed over a lot of good people to get all that money."

Taeva rested her chin in her hand, leaning against the bar. "He did?"

Before Grams could elaborate, the front door opened again.

Kellan walked in, cheeks and the tip of his nose flushed from the cold. He still wore his grey ensemble under his black coat, his lute in its case on his back. Like earlier, he looked to the bar as soon as he came in and grinned when he met Taeva's gaze.

She couldn't help but smile back. Grams elbowed her in the ribs, and she jumped, looking back to the older woman, eyes wide with alarm.

Grams winked. "Why don't you two go practice out back? The florist moved some of their plants and set out a fire ring. It'll be nice out there. I'll lock up in here as soon as these folks leave."

"That sounds great!" Kellan said, drawing up to the

other side of the bar. "Are you sure you can spare her? I'm happy to wait."

Grams snorted. "If I can't handle a few customers, you might as well start digging my grave."

"Grams," Taeva drawled, exasperated.

"Go *on*, sugar. Go practice so you'll be ready to play in here again. We're all looking forward to it."

Taeva paused as she grabbed her violin case from behind the bar. "All of you?" she asked.

"Yes, even your stubborn father," Grams answered with an exaggerated eye roll. "Now quit making this young man wait. Out, out!"

Heart in her throat, Taeva pulled her case to her chest and made her way to where Kellan waited by the back exit. He held her violin for her while she shrugged into her coat and scarf, then opened the door for her, placing his hand on her back as she passed through in front of him. She could feel the warmth of it even through all her layers of linen and wool.

"How did your gig go?" she asked.

"Great! I don't think people will ever get tired of Miralea's lights. I could make noise with the lute instead of music, and I don't think they'd notice."

"They come to hear you. The lights are extra," Taeva said. "At least that's how I feel about it."

"You might be a little biased. I hope you are, anyway."

He added the last sentence so softly, Taeva wasn't sure she was meant to hear it. It drew her up short, and she stood awkwardly in the middle of the shared patio. The florist had rearranged things to accommodate a metal fire ring, like Grams said, and the space felt even more enclosed and private than before. They stared at each other, the moment stretching taut between them. Her gaze dropped to his mouth again, the soft curve of his lips twisting something in her chest in a way that was as sweet as it was painful.

Taeva summoned every bit of her courage and said, "I'm very biased."

Tension melted out of Kellan as soon as the words left her, and he took a step toward her.

A gust of frigid late-autumn wind cut through the thin barrier of plants around them, and Taeva shivered, pulling her coat tighter around herself. Whatever moment they'd been having was broken. Again. She cursed the wind under her breath.

"We should get this fire going if we're planning on playing at all," Kellan said.

Coals still glowed in the fire pit, and Taeva put her case down on a nearby garden table and got to work stoking the fire while Kellan fed it more firewood. Before long, they had a warm flame burning, the wood crackling and popping.

The tense and awkward feeling between them returned as they worked on the fire and persisted as they pulled out and readied their instruments. To Taeva, it was like they were both dancing around each other, too scared to move in any closer. She was almost certain he'd welcome her if she made the first move, but what if she'd misread all the signs? What if he didn't like bold women? On the other hand, what if he was waiting for her to take the first step? She was so scared of ruining everything that she was paralyzed into inaction.

She blew into her hands, trying to warm them, and watched as he finished tuning the many strings on his lute. He glanced up at her, a rakish half-smile tipping up the right side of his lips. Maybe she should risk rejection to know for certain. The ache of not knowing was becoming too much to bear.

"There," he said, making one final adjustment to his highest string. "What do you want to play?"

Squaring her shoulders and gathering all the courage of a true bard and adventurer, Taeva answered, "I was hoping I could play something for you first and get your opinion."

Kellan's surprised smile was a reward in and of itself. "Absolutely!"

Taeva stood, drawing in a long, slow breath, then exhaled as she checked her tuning one more time. Then, closing her eyes, she started the first bar of "A Bright Love in Midwinter." The song told the story of a traveling knight who, while injured and recovering in a small town, found his true love in the cleric who healed him. She hoped he knew the song and, though it wasn't winter yet, would understand what she was trying to convey.

A few times, the magic around them tried to rise to the call of her music, but she pushed it aside with practiced ease before it could distract her. The notes fell easily from her fingers and bow, her only struggle being the scarf she'd mistakenly put on. She couldn't quite secure her violin under her chin how she wanted, so she had to settle for a thinner vibrato, but she thought it lent a nice softness to the music. She hoped Kellan would agree.

Finally, as she held the last note of the song, she opened her eyes. Kellan watched her, his lips slightly parted and an unreadable gleam in his eyes. Lowering her violin and bow, she waited for his critique.

"Taeva, I..." He put his lute in one of the nearby chairs and stood.

"I know. It needed more emotion, but this scarf got in the way." She tugged at it awkwardly, bow still in her hand.

He crossed over to her in two long strides. He took the

scarf from her and started unwinding it, his dark eyes boring into hers.

"It was beautiful," he whispered. He dropped her scarf on the ground, then turned the collar of her coat up against the lingering chill. "Can you run through it again? I want to play along."

One of his hands lingered on her collar while the other slipped beneath it to cup the nape of her neck. Taeva's heart beat like a wildly swinging metronome. She swallowed and nodded, unable to find her words. Kellan's rakish smirk was back, and suddenly Taeva could look at nothing but his mouth.

"One thing first," he whispered.

His lips pressed against hers, warm and somehow soft and firm all at the same time. She melted against him, and his hand left her collar to wrap around her waist and pull her closer. It was better, *more,* than any of her stories had led her to believe. The kiss and the warmth of his body sent a tingling awareness through her. She thought her hands might have been shaking, but she was too wrapped up in the tender way that he touched her to know for sure.

All too soon, he pulled away, the grin on his face almost wicked. "I've been wanting to do that for a while," he confessed.

Taeva answered with a grin of her own and, violin and bow still awkwardly in her hands, wrapped her arms around him and kissed him again. He smiled against her lips, then kissed her back. Thoroughly.

*T*aeva and Kellan stayed out on the patio until it was entirely too late, but she still sprang out of bed the next morning like she'd drank an energy potion.

There'd been more kissing, yes, but eventually they'd gotten around to the musical part of the evening. It had gone every bit as well as the kissing, which Taeva thought deserved another encore. She hummed the melody to "A Bright Love in Midwinter" as she dressed, picking her favorite blue and cream skirt and bodice for the day. She was twirling across the tavern floor, on her way to unlock the doors, when her family came down the stairs. She froze mid-turn, her skirt flaring and wrapping around her.

Grams's smirk was positively fiendish. "What's got you in such a good mood, sugar?"

Elawin gave an exaggerated gasp. "That lutist?"

"I don't want to hear this..." Tirson murmured, but he was smiling as he vanished into the kitchen on his way to the cellar.

Grams waved after him dismissively, then fluttered her hands at Taeva, urging her to hurry up. Taeva unlocked the doors and rejoined them at the bar, the blush on her cheeks even hotter than the fire she built a few moments before.

"Did he finally kiss you?" Grams said in a stage whisper.

Taeva blushed even more.

"He did!" Elawin said. "He better have been a gentleman about it."

"Oh, goddesses," Taeva said, burying her face in her apron. "He was. Absolutely. He would never... He's wonderful—"

The front doors opened before she could finish defending Kellan's honor, letting in the postman. Taeva hurried to collect the day's mail, delight running through her to see her name written in Kellan's hand on another of the letters.

"It's so adorable that he writes to you," Grams said as she passed Taeva on her way to the door. She handed the postman another scone. "Stay warm, Lyr."

Taeva's chest warmed as she put the rest of the mail on the table in the kitchen. Grams would take care of the entire city if she could. She'd know all their business if it was possible, too. Taeva finished tying on her apron, then ducked off into Leena's corner to read Kellan's letter before their first patrons arrived for the day.

*T*AEVA,

Last night was magical. YOU are magical. I don't know when you did it—or how—but I think you put on a spell on me. And I don't mind.

I'll be by later today. I can't wait to see you again.
Kellan

"IS THERE ANYONE IN THIS PLACE WHO CAN TAKE MY DAMNED order?"

Taeva looked up from the letter with a start to see an older woman at the bar. She shrugged off her coat—it looked finely tailored even from across the tavern—and glared at everything in the room like the decor itself had insulted her family.

"I'm sorry for the wait!" Taeva said as she tucked the letter into her pocket and scurried across the room to the back of the bar. "What can I get for you?"

The woman launched into such a nit-picky series of questions it left Taeva wondering if she'd ever eaten anywhere and actually enjoyed it. Was the beef in their meatloaf ever fed grain, or were they ever corralled? Where did the vegetables come from, and were they purely heirloom? Were the apples used for the cider pressed or squeezed?

Taeva didn't even have half the answers the woman wanted and eventually sent her off to her table in a huff, nonalcoholic cider in hand. Taeva wished it was still a little bitter, so it would match the woman's attitude. She wasn't truly bothered, though. Nothing could ruin her good mood. Not after last night and with the promise of another visit on the horizon.

The lunch crowd piled in, and she lost herself in the familiar hustle. The tavern got fairly crowded, almost all of the tables filled, but the lightness stayed in Taeva's step. The smiles she gave their customers came easier than they ever had since she'd returned home from her misadventure. Time breezed by in a blur of habitual work and anticipation.

The lunch rush was starting to taper off, and Taeva was dropping the last order off to a group of masons with dust in their hair, when she got the distinct feeling that she was being watched. The back of her neck prickled as she set the last plate down, thanking the lunch-goers.

It's the cranky woman again, back to complain more and glaring daggers at me, she thought, turning.

The Sage Reavers stood, frozen, as the door closed behind them, all three of them staring at her like they'd seen a ghost.

Every drop of blood drained from Taeva's face, and the warmth left her just as quickly, like she'd been doused with a bucket full of ice water. Even Mert was with them—a dwarf again, no longer a frog, like Miralea had said. He narrowed his eyes on her. Taeva wished the moment had finally come when the earth would comply and swallow her whole. Anything to get out from under that hateful gaze.

Heathric, a mountain of a man who looked even larger standing in their quaint tavern, regained his composure first. He gave her a smile that was more of a grimace than anything pleasant and gestured toward an empty table near the door. The Reavers walked over to it, chain shirts and sword belts clinking. Heathric didn't take his eyes off her as he took his seat. She stood rooted in place, and he lifted a brow expectantly. The scar that ran through it caught her eye, and she gulped.

Since the ground wasn't going to help, she gave serious thought to running. But, as her heartbeat sped away without her, she realized she didn't have anywhere to go. If Miralea was wrong and they had come looking for her, they would eventually find her again. So she took a deep breath and imagined she was walking on stage. She was scared, but she knew how to regulate that emotion better than she had when she'd last seen the Reavers. She kept her serving tray in front of her like a shield, but she walked toward them, and her strides didn't falter.

"Have a seat, Taeva," Heathric said, kicking out the chair across from him.

Taeva eased into the seat, perching on the edge. Lily and Mert sat to either side, Lily studying her with a carefully blank expression. Mert looked like he could barely contain his fury, his face a blotchy red under his dark beard.

"You didn't tell us your family owned a tavern," Heathric said.

Fear lanced through Taeva, and her fingers squeezed the tray until her knuckles were white. They hadn't only found her; they knew her family was here too. She didn't think they were the type of band to hurt people's families, but could she even say she knew them? She'd only traveled with them for a week before the incident.

"It—" Her voice caught, and she paused to clear her throat. Her next words came out sounding braver than she felt. "It's not very impressive for an adventurer to say they grew up working in a tavern."

Lily scoffed and flicked her pale hair over her shoulder. "I was a seamstress."

"Scribe," Heathric volunteered.

"It doesn't matter what yeh were before. What matters is yeh turned me into a goddess-be-damned frog!" Mert growled.

Taeva flinched back, eyes wide. Unconsciously, she lifted her make-shift shield, ready to deflect a blow.

Mert glared at her for another few heartbeats, then dissolved into laughter. "It was damned funny! After the fact, mind."

Lily giggled. "Oh, your face! He really scared you, huh?"

Heathric shook his head, the expression on his face somewhere between indulgent and annoyed. "Satisfied?"

"Yeah, I reckon," Mert said, wiping tears of laughter out of his beard.

"He wouldn't agree to come in here unless he got to do that," Lily said, still grinning.

Taeva lowered her tray. "He... What?"

"Ha, the face ya made! Had to tease ya, lass!"

Heathric snorted. "We had to track you down to pay you. He had a fit when I tried to tell him he couldn't pull his little stunt."

Taeva blinked at Heathric, confused. "Pay?" she squeaked.

"That's what I said." Heathric pulled a small coin pouch off his belt and tossed it across the table to her. It landed with a metallic jingle. "We deducted what it cost to have Mert turned back, but otherwise, it's the share we originally agreed to."

"But I almost ruined the whole thing! I could have gotten us killed," Taeva argued. She eyed the coin pouch like it was viper, coiled to strike.

"That's called a mistake, aye," Mert said. "It can happen to anyone. Just more dangerous in our line o' work."

"You were all so mad. And I lied about my experience," Taeva continued, her voice growing weaker as her arguments continued. She'd spent all these months thinking the Reavers hated her. It was hard to come to terms with the smiling adventurers sitting around the table now.

"Of course we were!" Lily said. "We didn't expect such a rookie mistake. But we calmed down after we got Mert back to normal. And we were all rookies once."

"Take the coin," Heathric said. "We did still finish the job, and your spells before the frog one helped."

Taeva finally took the coin pouch, her hand shaking as she reached for it. Even with the coin they'd removed, there was enough left in the purse for it to clink satisfyingly.

"I thought you were all here for revenge," Taeva admitted.

"Revenge? Goddesses fend," Lily groaned.

"Surely ya know us better than all that," said Mert.

"To be clear," Heathric added, "we aren't here to rehire you. You need more actual experience on some smaller jobs. But we aren't the type to seek revenge for a mistake. It's against Reaver code."

"Oh. The code," Taeva said. She had never heard their code since she was a new, and ultimately temporary, hire.

"Right," Mert clapped his hands, making Taeva jump. He snickered, then continued. "Time for food and some drinks!"

"Can we order with you, or do we need to go up to the bar?" Heathric asked.

Taeva opened her mouth, ready to tell them to go back up to the bar and order with Grams, who was currently manning the coin box, but her protest died on her lips.

"I'll take your orders here," she said, forgoing their usual procedure. She felt like the Reavers had done the same for her, but on a much bigger scale.

And she was endlessly grateful.

aeva handled the Reavers' orders, feeling light as air again. It was a different kind of lightness than how she'd felt when she woke that morning. Her relief deepened, like her dread over the Reavers had taken up so much space inside her that she hadn't been able to feel other things as clearly. Now that it was gone, her joy from earlier in the morning could fill her more completely.

Her heart positively sang as she worked through the rest of their lunch crowd. The Reavers stayed, ordering another round and spreading a map out across the table. Taeva tried not to pay it too much mind when she delivered their fresh mugs of mead, but she got caught glancing at it anyway. Mert winked at her when he noticed, and she flushed with guilt as she quickly looked away. None of them said anything about it.

As the afternoon lull set in, Taeva settled behind the counter with her mother and pulled out her violin. The cold air wasn't the best for the wood or the hide glue holding it all together. After spending so long playing outside the night before, she wanted to check for any cracks or split seams.

Elawin smiled as Taeva tightened her bow to give it a quick once-over before taking out the instrument itself.

"It's been so good to hear you playing again," she said.

Taeva sat the bow on the counter and pulled the silk

cloth off her violin. "It's been good to play again," she answered. "Really, really good."

Her mother was quiet for a moment, picking at a loose thread on one of her sleeves. Tension framed her, like the wood holding a painter's canvas taut. Taeva paused, violin resting in her lap.

"Is everything alright?"

Elawin sighed. "I want you to know we're all very proud of you. And if the violin takes you away from the tavern, we won't argue against it. We've seen you coming back to life over the last few weeks, and we don't want anything to stop that. Even your father. That's why he orchestrated that whole thing with the cider. He knew you would figure out a way to fix it, and he was hoping it would give you the little push you needed. We want you to follow your heart wherever it takes you, though we'd rather you didn't go too far." She finished with a weak laugh.

Tears welled behind Taeva's eyes. She'd never expected so much support from either of her parents—especially not for her father to ruin a batch of cider just to try to steer her back toward playing. She'd been prepared to fight them every step of the way, like she'd been doing ever since her playing got more serious when she was a teenager. Her mother's words plucked at her heartstrings like they wanted to make their own music. She blinked and looked up, fanning her face and hoping the tears didn't land on her violin and possibly mar the varnish.

"I don't want to go very far," she said. "And maybe with Leena's help, I can work on getting the hang of some of the business things. I want to try to find a good balance."

Elawin blinked back tears of her own as she tucked a stray curl behind Taeva's ear. "Balance will be just right."

Before either of them could dissolve further into tears,

the front door opened. Head Watchmen Tybrecht Wolfstone walked in, closely followed by some of their regular Watchman patrons—Groslig, Torressa, and Len.

Tybrecht looked like a new man now that all the stress of the investigation had been lifted from his shoulders. The dark circles under his eyes were less like bruises, and his salt-and-pepper hair was neatly combed. He smiled at Taeva and her mother as he walked in, and it reached his eyes. He was refreshed. Unburdened.

"The man of the year!" Tirson said. He walked out of the kitchen, sleeves rolled up like always. He reached across the counter to shake Tybrecht's hand. "Give this man and his Watchmen anything they want on the house."

"Why, thank you, Goldmead," Tybrecht said, looking pleased. "Autumn mead?" he asked, looking back towards the other Watchmen.

"Yes, please," Groslig said as the other two nodded.

Taeva sat her violin down next to her bow and jumped up to help her mother pour drinks.

"You know," Tirson said, "if you're interested, I can take you to the cellar and show you a little bit of the process behind making that mead. A private tour, also on the house!"

Taeva snorted a laugh as she set the first filled mug aside and started another. Her father would give anyone who asked a private tour. Fortunately, he was so often busy in the cellar that he wasn't in the main room enough to pester people about it.

"Going to show us all the secret ingredients, eh?" Tybrecht asked.

"Absolutely not," Tirson said with a chuckle. "Only one of them."

Tybrecht barked a laugh. "Well, let me look the part."

As Taeva put his mug of mead on the bar in front of him, he shrugged out of his coat, unbuttoned the cuffs of his sleeves, and started to roll them up to his elbows to match Tirson. As he rolled up his right sleeve, he revealed a fresh scar that ran from his wrist almost all the way to his elbow. The skin was puckered and red, only recently healed. Taeva's eyes widened. The edges were a sickly green, the veins around the wound pronounced. They were such a bright green it looked like roots had wormed their way into his skin.

And he reached for his mead with his left hand.

"It was you!" Taeva blurted, pointing at the half-healed wound on his arm.

Tybrecht froze. The Watchmen beside him at the bar jerked to attention. The entire tavern seemed to hold its breath as all eyes fell on her, heavy with expectation.

"That wound can't be much more than a month old and is clearly full of distilled basilisk poison. And you're left-handed! You killed Lord Amberwood!"

Tybrecht scoffed. "Your daughter has a vivid imagination, Goldmead."

"I saw all that blood on the floor in your house the morning after. I went there to report to you, but you already knew," Torressa said, her voice measured. She slowly set her mug back on the bar and eased her hand towards her sword. "I dismissed it—thought it was just another day on a dangerous job—but it was you. And you weren't sick. You were poisoned!"

The tension in the room broke with a crash. Tybrecht hurled his mug at Torressa, and glass burst against the edge of her blade as she drew it, blocking in the same smooth movement. Mead splashed all over the tall elf, and sharp pieces of the mug clattered across the floor and bar top.

Tybrecht dropped his shoulder and plowed into Torressa. Her feet slid out from underneath her, the floor slippery thanks to the mead, and she went down hard.

Tybrecht shot toward the door, his hand on his own sword. He grabbed bar stools and flung them to the ground as he ran. Groslig tripped over one and went tumbling to the floor. He grabbed at Len as he went, fighting for balance, and the half-orc and the human both went down in a heap.

Tybrecht had as good as escaped. He was halfway to the door, and all the other Watchmen were on the ground. Len was dazed. He fought to lift himself up on one elbow, his eyes unfocused.

But Taeva could stop him. Between one of Tybrecht's running steps and the next, she snatched up her violin and her bow. Miralea said all it would take was a scale, and Taeva had tested that theory with good results. She warmed up with scales. She had for years. She could run through them in her sleep.

She picked C major. Simple. Strong. The magic surged to her with the first note she pulled from the strings, but this time she didn't push it away. Instead, she pictured the outcome she wanted, focused on making the magic real and solid as she strung the notes together.

The magic leapt to her command, shaping itself with the clear vibrations of her violin. Thick cords of dark green light sprang up from the floor and banded around Tybrecht's legs. They snaked up to his torso as Taeva finished the octave. The murderer strained against her magic, but she had willed the vines to be unbreakable, and her will was stronger than Tybrecht's. They held firm.

Taeva lowered her bow, fingers still tingling with the surge of magic. Her thoughts whirled through the entire gamut of emotions—from the fear that speared through her upon realizing Tybrecht was the killer, the sheer anxiety of using magic again, and pride in herself for catching him. She didn't know what feeling to focus on and which ones she needed to put back into the dark corner, so she plopped down on the closest stool, overwhelmed.

"Goddesses," she muttered.

"Damnit! Let me go! You don't have anything on me!" Tybrecht bellowed. "This is ridiculous!"

Torressa grabbed hold of the bar and pulled herself back up. "Why'd you run, then?" she asked, putting a hand to her ribs. She turned to her partners. "How's Len?"

Groslig shuffled across the floor to check on the dazed human. "How many fingers?"

Len shoved his hand away. "Three. I took a hit. It didn't make me incapable of counting, you oaf."

"He's perfectly normal," Groslig declared.

"Good," Torressa said. She pulled a set of manacles off her belt and walked over to Tybrecht. Grabbing one of his arms, she twisted it around his back. "As I'm sure you've realized, you're under arrest. Other arm, please."

All the fight seemed to drain out of him then, and he complied. Torressa locked his arms in place, then turned back toward Taeva, keeping her hands on the chains holding Tybrecht captive.

The Watchwoman smiled, and it freed something up in the rest of the room. Suddenly, everyone was talking at once. They rushed to Taeva, hugging her while she awkwardly lifted her violin and bow out of the way, trying to keep them from being crushed. She couldn't look away from the glowing vines of magic she'd created. Slowly, the truth of what she'd done crept over her. She'd caught him. She'd saved the day.

Then she looked to the corner, where the Sage Reavers

sat. They'd all stood, prepared to give chase themselves, and all regarded her with calculating eyes. Heathric smiled and raised his mug toward her in salute.

Taeva took great pride in herself for meeting his eyes and smiling back. She didn't even blush.

*M*iralea played the lead like she normally did, each note coming from her flute with crisp precision. Her ribbons of light fluttered through The Honey Goblet, twining through the dancers and looping through the tables. Kellan sat on a stool, foot tapping a drum while he played chords on his lute and held the rhythm.

And Taeva, playing second fiddle to the flute, added her own magic. She kept it simple—tiny orbs of light that flared and faded in the rafters like the twinkling of stars. She held the idea of them firmly in her mind as she played the simpler part, not an ounce of tension in her tone. They'd practiced the piece and the magics together the night before, and though she was nervous when she'd first stepped on stage, she'd settled back into the groove of performing with more ease than she'd expected. It felt natural.

The piece drew to a close, taking the magic with it. Kellan stood up and leaned his lute against the wall. "We're going to take a short break, everyone, but we've got more music for you, don't worry," he announced to the tavern, eliciting another round of enthusiastic applause.

Taeva stowed her violin back into its case, strapping it into place and latching the lid in case a rowdy patron jostled it. Kellan waited for her at the edge of the stage and offered her a hand as she stepped down. She took it, grinning like a fool, then grinning even harder when he leaned over and placed a kiss on her forehead.

"You were perfect," he said.

Her cheeks warmed. "Not even close."

"Perfect," he repeated, giving her hand a squeeze.

A familiar uniformed elf woman waved to them from the bar, then gestured for them to join her.

Torressa bore the Head Watchman title with ease. If she'd been stressed or overworked during the week of transition since Tybrecht's arrest, she hid it well. Her short hair was neatly styled, and her uniform clean and well pressed. She wore an easy smile as Taeva and Kellan walked up.

"Sounded good!" she said, setting a glass of cider down. "I meant to come in earlier to formally thank you, but I've been up to my neck in paperwork." She grimaced on the last word, her nose crinkling.

"You didn't need to worry," Taeva said. "I didn't do anything that obligated you to go out of your way."

"Yes, she did," Leena said at Taeva's elbow. She hadn't even seen the other woman leave her corner.

"You did way more than I did," Taeva argued.

"You *all* did the real heavy lifting in the investigation, unorthodox as it was. Damn shame that all of us missed what was so clear to you," Torressa said.

Leena put her hands on her hips. "We're available for consultations if you need us."

Taeva whipped her head toward Leena so quickly her hair smacked Kellan in the face. He laughed, brushing it away.

Torressa gave Leena an indulgent smile. "I'll have to keep that in mind."

"I still can't believe he did it," Kellan said. "I thought he was such a good man."

"We all did. It's probably why we were so blind toward him," Torressa said. "What's even worse is he did it to help us. Misguided, but that was his reason."

Taeva's jaw dropped. "The Watch," she said.

Torressa nodded. "Yep. He figured if Amberwood was dead, he couldn't buy out the Watch, and we'd all keep our jobs. Became the very murderous schemer we're sworn to protect people against. Bastard." She took a sip of her drink, brow furrowed. "On a lighter note, did you hear about the tourney?"

Taeva and the others glanced at each other, all shaking their heads, so she continued.

"Silversage was released as soon as the trail for Wolfstone was over, but he's still furious. Understandable. The king's trying to make it up to him with a tourney in his honor. I'm sure you'll all be getting formal invitations as guests of honor soon. You should consider performing, too," she said, gesturing towards Taeva and Kellan.

"She would love to perform!" Leena declared without waiting for Taeva to answer.

"She would?" Taeva asked. Her voice pitched up in a question, but she glared at her friend, willing her to drop the subject.

"Yes. And everyone will love it. Because you're great."

"And I'll be glad to join," Kellan said. "I'm sure I could rope Miralea into it too."

The other bard watched them from the stage, her brow furrowed like she knew they were talking about her.

"Probably," Kellan added.

Torressa drained the last bit of cider from her glass and set it on the bar. "I doubt the tourney will make Silversage feel any better, between our bumbling investigation and his wife being sick, but if you all play, at least we know the entertainment will be top-notch." She stood up, pulling her uniform straight. "Back to work. Almost time to call it a night. See you at the tourney."

She gave them a quick salute before slipping through the crowd and out the door. Taeva waved as she left, smiling as she watched a few other Watchmen pull out of the crowd to accompany their new boss.

"I'm so proud of her. She deserved that promotion," she said.

"She did always strike me as the most competent of the bunch," Leena agreed. "And the rest of the Watch likes her. She was the natural choice."

Taeva rounded the bar to pour them drinks. They were quiet for a moment while she worked, her back toward them. She poured four mugs of the autumn mead, intending to bring one over to Miralea when they returned to the stage.

"Have you heard from your Reaver friends again?" Leena asked as soon as Taeva turned around.

"Actually, yes." She set the mugs in front of her friends and pulled her own closer. She looked at the golden mead, reluctant to tell them about the second meeting. "They offered me a job. Nothing big, not a dangerous contract, but after I caught Tybrecht, they figured I could handle more work."

"Of course you can," Kellan said. He sounded happy, but Taeva had spent enough time with him that she could recognize the strain in his expression. He wasn't as thrilled with the idea as he was letting on. "Are you going to go with them?"

Taeva met his eyes, then Leena's, then looked around the tavern. "Not this time."

Kellan and Leena both melted a little, relieved. Kellan's

face lit up with true joy this time, and Leena nudged him with her shoulder.

Taeva looked at them both, her heart full to bursting. "I need to practice more. And I can't think of a better place to be than here."

Leena raised her mug. "A toast! To unharried practice and the healing power of home!"

Taeva lifted her drink, and they clinked their mugs together with gusto. Then she drank deep.

It tasted wonderful.

ACKNOWLEDGMENTS

Here we are again! A fourth book finished. I feel so lucky that I have the support I need to get things like this done—it's a little insane.

Thank you to my fabulous beta readers who took an early look at this and gave me such wonderful feedback! You're all so brilliant and talented and skilled. I'm so lucky to know all of you! How I managed to surround myself with so many incredible artists is beyond me.

David- Dude, you are so cool! Thank you for taking the time to read this between your many, many epic projects. Keep shredding, death metal bard!

Nirav- A fabulous artist and one of the truest champions of art I've had the privilege to interact with. Thank you for cheering so loudly, not just for me, but for so many other indie authors! We need more people like you in this world.

Max- Listen. You already know how awesome you are. Drawing, music, writing—there's literally nothing you can't do! Thank you for boosting me up and always being willing to listen to my unhinged rants.

Megan- Everyone needs a true ride-or-die friend like you. Thank you for your endless support, for living in delulu with me, for having my back when things are chaotic, and also for knocking me upside the head when I need it. You're amazing! Never change!

ABOUT THE AUTHOR

Sam Parrish was born and raised in the woods of central Florida. When she isn't working or writing, she enjoys playing music, camping, and fly fishing. She still lives in Florida (despite her escape efforts) with her husband and their menagerie of animals.